"I really can't make it," Jessica said. "Sorry, Nancy. I was just on my way somewhere. I'll get my uniform from you at school tomorrow."

Nancy's voice turned menacing. "I think you'd better get into this car now, Claire," the cheerleading adviser warned.

Claire?

"You have to be with the other girls," Nancy said in the same cold voice. "We can't do it without you."

Jessica was bewildered. "What is going on—" Suddenly she noticed Lila's pallor and Annie's enormous eyes. There was something very wrong here. Her friends were terrified.

"Run, Jessica!" Lila screamed.

SWEET VALLEY High.

"R" FOR REVENGE

Written by
Kate William

Created by
FRANCINE PASCAL

BANTAM BOOKS
NEW YORK · TORONTO · LONDON · SYDNEY · AUCKLAND

SWEET VALLEY HIGH
SUPER THRILLER: "R" FOR REVENGE
A BANTAM BOOK : 0 553 506188

Originally published in U.S.A. by Bantam Books

First publication in Great Britain

PRINTING HISTORY
Bantam edition published 1998

Conceived by Francine Pascal

Produced by Daniel Weiss Associates, Inc,
33 West 17th Street, New York, NY 10011

Bantam Books are published by Transworld Publishers Ltd,
61–63 Uxbridge Road, London W5 5SA,
in Australia by Transworld Publishers (Australia) Pty Ltd,
15–25 Helles Avenue, Moorebank, NSW 2170,
and in New Zealand by Transworld Publishers (NZ) Ltd,
3 William Pickering Drive, Albany, Auckland.

Printed and bound in Great Britain by
Cox & Wyman Ltd, Reading, Berkshire.

To Diana McNelis

Prologue

Upstairs, the stereo was blasting. The basement room was dim, but with each beat of the music Jessica Wakefield could make out a glimmer of ripples disturbing the surface of the chilly water she was standing in. Percussion vibrated the house and thrummed through her body, reaching deep within her to jar her cold, damp bones.

Jessica's ankles were tied to the base of a metal pillar, deep under the black water. Her hands were tied behind her back, bound to the same pillar. The water level was rising. First it had covered her sneakers and goose-pimpled legs. Now it was at hip level, saturating the miniskirt of her cheerleading uniform.

She struggled again with the rope that bound her wrists. Jessica was afraid that trying to loosen the sinewy cord was as useless as trying to make

1

out more than an occasional line of words in the music that beat down on her from above. But she couldn't stop herself. Giving in to the rope meant accepting her own helplessness, and that was one thing Jessica refused to do.

Besides, she reasoned, concentrating on the rope and the rock song might keep her from thinking about the black water that swirled ominously around her, its level rising little by little every second.

She recognized the song. Of course, she usually listened to nothing but the newest, trendiest music. But this was a song she'd heard on the oldies station her twin sister, Elizabeth, sometimes insisted on. *Lynyrd Skynyrd,* Jessica recalled suddenly. And the song really rocked, in an old-fashioned sort of way. The instruments seemed to echo wetly against the cold cement walls and the swelling tide.

"I'm as free as a bird now," the band was singing.

"Free? Don't I *wish!*" Jessica whispered grimly, feeling the ropes slicing into her wrists as she twisted her hands in another futile effort to free herself.

Her comment went unnoticed. It was muffled by the trickle of water, the insistent music, and the desperate whimpering of seven other high-school cheerleaders who huddled in the basement with her, all bound at the wrists and ankles. Annie Whitman was tied to the same pillar as Jessica, back-to-back with her. Jessica could feel tension radiating from Annie, and she could hear an occasional muffled cry.

From a far corner of the room she recognized the pitiful sobs of Heather Mallone. Heather was a senior, a year ahead of Jessica. And like Jessica, she was a cocaptain of the Sweet Valley High cheerleading squad. Now the shapely blonde was tied to a pipe from which a spigot was gushing cold, dark water into the room—in the corner where the uneven cement floor was the lowest. *Heather must be wetter than any of us,* Jessica thought. Normally she resented her bossy, manipulative cocaptain. Now she felt sorry for her.

A soft voice nearby startled Jessica. "If you're thinking up a brilliant plan for getting us out of this," suggested Lila Fowler, "now would be an awesome time to unveil it."

Jessica looked over her right shoulder to where her best friend stood against a cement wall, tightly tied. Lila spoke low enough so nobody else could hear her above the long guitar solo that showered down on the cheerleaders from above. Her voice was steady. But her brown eyes stared at Jessica out of the darkness, huge and scared, rimmed with dark streaks of eyeliner. Lila's long, light brown hair usually gleamed like satin. Now it looked as damp and stringy as Jessica's felt against her shoulders. Jessica was glad there was no mirror nearby. For both girls it was a major bad-hair day.

Jessica knew Lila didn't expect an answer, so she only gazed back at her, silently thanking her friend for not crying like the others. If cool, elegant Lila were to break down, Jessica might lose it too. For now, she wouldn't cry. She was too angry, scared, and frustrated for tears. Despite her reputation as a brilliant schemer who could find a way out of any disaster, Jessica had no idea how to escape the rising water.

And nobody else outside of this house knew where they were.

In a few hours she and the other girls would drown.

"Why didn't I see this coming?" she demanded of herself in a soft, accusing whisper. "Why didn't I see the truth from the very start?"

Chapter 1

Jessica Wakefield stepped on her best friend's back.

"Watch it!" Lila Fowler growled. "It's bad enough I'm on my hands and knees in the middle of the football field on a beautiful Wednesday afternoon when I could be—*should* be—sunbathing by my pool. Do you have to *step* on me too?"

"Sorry," Jessica said contritely. But she wasn't. She took a perverse pleasure out of seeing her wealthy, sophisticated best friend crouching in the dirt with herself and Maria Santelli balancing on top of her—even if it *was* for a cheerleading formation.

"Any day now, Jessica," Amy Sutton reminded her, bent over on the ground next to Lila. "*You're* the one who wanted to be on top of the pyramid. You know, the craving for that kind of attention can be a sign of insecurity—"

"Stop with the Project Youth psychobabble!" Jessica begged. "Ever since you've been working at that hot line, you psychoanalyze all of us like you're Sigmund Freud!"

"Sigmund!" Maria said with a laugh. "Growing up with a name like that, it's no wonder the guy was a master of insecurities."

"Girls, we all know about Jessica's many neuroses," called Heather Mallone, standing beside the unfinished human pyramid. "But we're here to practice cheerleading, not psychology. Cut the chatter and get to work!"

Jessica felt Lila's shoulder stiffen under her foot. She and Lila might be worst rivals as well as best friends, but when it came to Heather Mallone, they were in complete agreement. They *loathed* her.

"Are we having fun yet?" asked Patty Gilbert, obviously hoping to break the tension. Patty was an expert dancer and choreographer, but now she was lined up beside Amy on the field, her hands and knees on the damp earth.

"I think my foot's falling asleep," complained sophomore Annie Whitman from her spot on the second tier of the pyramid, next to Maria.

"Focus, girls!" Heather ordered. She ran a hand through her long blond curls, tapping her foot impatiently in her custom-made cheerleading shoes.

Jessica clenched her jaw and narrowed her blue-green eyes. She would have been perfectly happy

6

to be sole captain of the cheerleading squad when her last cocaptain, Robin Wilson, announced she was moving to Denver. But then Heather had arrived in Sweet Valley, marking the start of a rotten time Jessica still thought of as the Pom-pom Wars.

Heather had schemed to steal Jessica's squad away and had actually succeeded! Eventually the two were forced to work together to compete in the regional cheer-off. Since then they'd settled in as cocaptains, but their coexistence was anything but peaceful.

"Jessica," Heather continued, "if you're not athletic enough to climb to the top of the pyramid, get off and we'll put Jade up there." She gestured toward tiny, black-haired Jade Wu, who was on the ground with her, acting as spotter for the pyramid. "Or *me*," Heather finished with a smile.

Maria and Annie, on their knees on top of Lila, Patty, and Amy, hunched down slightly so that Jessica could climb onto their shoulders. But Jessica was busy glaring daggers at Heather.

"And now, ladies and gentlemen," Lila began in a television-announcer voice. *"We welcome you to another endless edition of* The Jessica and Heather Show!"

"Well, you *are* kind of *heavy* to be on top," Heather pointed out to Jessica.

Jessica looked down her nose at her cocaptain. "I know it's *difficult* for someone with your *limited brain capacity* to remember things," she said with mock sympathy to Heather. "But get a clue! I have to be on top of the pyramid because we agreed I would try my new dismount today!" She desperately wished it was Heather instead of Lila underneath her foot. She would have *loved* to step on her smug, perfectly coifed, pointy little head.

"I don't see what was wrong with the dismount I choreographed for Jade," Heather argued. "The crowd loved it at the field hockey game last week."

"The Jessica and Heather Show, *where cheerleading meets professional wrestling—,*" Amy continued.

"There's nothing *wrong* with your dismount, exactly," Jessica told Heather, smiling sweetly as she climbed onto Annie and Maria's shoulders. "Except that it's *boring.* But of course that doesn't surprise me, considering the source. . . ."

"And I suppose you can do better?" Heather asked Jessica, hands on her slim hips.

"*Where insults fly as fast as double cartwheels, and the pom-pom is mightier than the sword!*" Maria called out, continuing the mock TV announcement.

"Watch me and see," Jessica said confidently. "Maybe you'll pick up a few pointers."

"*In today's episode,*" intoned Patty, "*we again explore the question: Can two blond cocaptains share a cheerleading squad—without committing teenacide?*"

"Everyone shut up and cheer!" Heather yelled.

"This is what I love about cheerleading," Annie muttered. "The way we're all one big happy family—"

"A *dysfunctional* one—," Amy added.

"With a terminal case of sibling rivalry," Lila finished.

Jessica rose halfway, one knee on Maria's shoulder and one on Annie's. She took a deep breath, smoothed the front of her hot-pink shorts, and prepared to stand.

"Watch it, Jess!" Maria hissed as Jessica's foot caught her shoulder blade. The pyramid swayed, but Jessica barely noticed.

"I *am* watching," Jessica breathed. But she wasn't watching Maria. She steadied herself, and the three tiers of cheerleaders stabilized. From the sudden catching of breath beneath her, Jessica knew she wasn't the only cheerleader who'd noticed the source of her distraction.

A guy was walking along the sidelines of the football field—a tall, lean guy with glossy brown hair and a sexy walk.

Now we have something to cheer about! Jessica thought.

Who is that tall, dark, and hunky man? Lila wondered. *And why do I have to see him while I'm crouched on all fours, my hair dragging in the mud?* Above her, Maria shifted position, probably to get a better look, and her knee dug painfully into Lila's back. The brown-haired junior looked

9

small, but Lila was sure she weighed a ton.

Then there was Jessica. Lila knew exactly why the pyramid had swayed and nearly toppled. Jessica's hunk radar had kicked in. And Jessica always lost sight of everything else when confronted by a good-looking guy. Luckily her desire to impress him was stronger than her momentary distraction. Lila couldn't see her best friend, but she could imagine Jessica up there at the top of the pyramid, swinging her arms dramatically and showing off like a trained pup. It was disgusting. Lila could practically hear her salivating.

Unlike her best friend, Lila was too refined to be so obvious about her attraction to a guy. But this guy was definitely worth a second—subtle— look. And maybe a third. His straight brown hair was longer in the front. *Very stylish,* she thought. His shoulders were broad. And he wore a loose, plum-colored shirt that draped over his muscular arms like silk.

"Hunk alert!" Amy announced in a stage whisper, as if the other girls might not have noticed him. "*Major* hunk alert!"

"Right," Lila whispered, rolling her eyes. "Like he'll ever give you and me a second look after seeing us in the mud! I can feel my leggings getting dirtier by the second."

"What does it matter?" Patty asked reasonably. "You two aren't in the market. You've got boyfriends!"

Lila felt Amy's shoulder twitch. If the girls had been standing, Amy probably would have thrown up her arms in exasperation. Lila knew that Amy never did have much use for Patty. "Well, that's a blinding flash of the obvious," Amy said. "But there's no harm in checking out some new blood. I'm just *looking* at him, not marrying him!"

Amy had been dating senior Barry Rork, a tennis player, for ages. Lila's boyfriend, Bo—short for Beauregard Creighton the Third—lived in Washington, D.C., but both Lila and Bo could afford frequent long-distance phone calls and travel expenses. Bo was a total catch. Lila had known him only a few months, but she loved him. In fact, he was coming to visit in a few days, and Lila couldn't wait. Still, as Amy had said, there was nothing wrong with checking out other guys—from a distance, of course. Especially guys who looked as amazingly buff as the one who was walking along the sidelines.

"We *all* have steady boyfriends," Maria observed. "Except Jessica . . . and Heather, of course."

Heather whirled, her face turning pink. If not for the pyramid, Lila would have given Maria a high five.

"Focus, everyone!" Heather insisted, controlling her anger. But her pale eyes were focused on the tall, dark stranger.

*   *   *

11

Jessica posed gracefully as she scrutinized the brown-haired hunk from her vantage point on top of the pyramid. Always happiest in the limelight, she felt like she was on top of the world. Of course, being an identical twin gave Jessica plenty of opportunities to be the center of attention. But unlike her modest sister, Elizabeth, she never grew tired of being admired.

Most of the time Jessica didn't mind not having a steady boyfriend. It was more fun to have half the guys at school pining over her. But those were only immature high-school boys. This was a *man*—in his midtwenties, she guessed. She tilted her head to make sure her hair caught the late afternoon sunlight, waiting for him to notice her.

"You can do your little dismount any day now, Jessica," Heather prompted. "Or are you afraid of screwing it up?"

"Haven't you ever heard of a *dramatic pause?*" Jessica asked, staring thoughtfully at the good-looking stranger. He wore tight-fitting jeans. A complicated-looking camera was slung around his neck.

For an instant the camera reminded Jessica of Quentin Berg, the egotistical photographer at *Flair* fashion magazine, where Jessica and Elizabeth had been interns. Jessica had dated Quentin, hoping to jump-start a career as a model. But he'd turned out to be a worm—a good-looking worm, but a worm nonetheless. *Of course*, she decided charitably, *it wouldn't be fair to hold that against* all *cute photographers*.

When the stranger turned toward the cheerleaders, Heather bounded into the air to perform her signature move—a triple herky, ending in a Y leap. Jessica grimaced. The spectacular combination always caught people's attention—and Jessica's wrath.

"Show-off," Jessica muttered as Heather flew into another combination. Of all the irritating things about Heather, the most irritating of all was the fact that she really was a competent cheerleader. Jessica sighed. *OK, she's better than competent*, she admitted to herself. *A lot better.*

Why couldn't Heather be a klutz? Jessica wished. *If she wasn't so good at cheerleading, she never would have been able to force me off my own squad!* The cheerleaders had followed Heather only because she promised to get them to the championship. They even went along with a starvation diet, a sadistic exercise regime, and Heather's decision to kick Maria and Sandy Bacon off the squad because she said they weren't good enough.

The worst thing about the whole episode, in Jessica's opinion, was that Heather *had* managed to lead the squad to the national championship. Of course, that was only after Jessica created her own squad, with Maria, Sandy, and Lila on it, and the two groups eventually merged.

She sighed now to see the cute guy watching

one of Heather's dizzying jumps. Then she grinned. He'd raised his camera too late to capture her flashy move.

Here goes, Jessica thought. She raised her arms gracefully, waiting until she had the photographer's full attention. Then she catapulted herself into the air for her new dismount, complete with a flip and a perfect landing.

"Way to go, Jessica!" Lila exclaimed.

"You aced it!" called Jade.

Jessica glanced up, a dazzling smile on her face. She was certain the hunk had snapped at least one photograph. Now he was sure to remember her. "Heather Mallone, eat my pom-poms!" she whispered, wiping her hands on her shorts as her fellow cheerleaders broke formation and gathered around her to praise the new dismount. She looked up to see if the gorgeous photographer was still watching.

With a stab of annoyance Jessica realized for the first time that he wasn't alone. One of his two companions was a woman Jessica had never seen before. The other was all too familiar—down to the sun flashing off his bald head.

"So who is that babe-a-licious dude with Principal Cooper?" Heather asked thoughtfully. "Has anyone seen him around here before?"

Patty's huge brown eyes sparkled as she stretched out her calf muscles. "Chrome Dome never let on that he had friends who looked like that!"

Jessica didn't care if the hunk was standing on the sidelines with Chrome Dome Cooper. She usually ignored the principal's existence as much as possible. The source of her anxiety was the other visitor—a blond, glamorous woman who was obviously "with" the photographer. It looked as if the principal was taking them on a tour of the school grounds.

Jessica pulled Lila away from the other girls, and Amy followed. "Do you think they're a couple?" she asked as the principal led his two visitors onto the field toward the cheerleaders.

"Chrome Dome and the sophisticated woman?" Amy asked, her gray eyes twinkling mischievously.

"You know what I mean!" Jessica thundered, glaring at Amy dangerously. "Does it look like Mr. Right and the red Chanel suit are an item?"

Lila shrugged. "Since when would *that* stop you?"

"I don't think they're an item," Amy decided, wiping dirt off her bike shorts. "The woman is way old for him."

As the trio approached, Jessica realized Amy was right. The man was younger than she'd first guessed, maybe eighteen or twenty. And the woman was old—at least in her midthirties, maybe even her forties—but she still looked good, like an elegant movie star. As the girls watched, she stopped for a moment to scribble something in a notepad.

15

"The age difference doesn't mean anything," Lila pointed out. "Before my parents got back together, my father dated a lot of good-looking younger women, even a famous actress." Lila's parents had divorced when she was a baby. But they'd recently rediscovered each other and remarried. "Why shouldn't a successful older woman have a boy toy of her own?" Lila concluded with a shrug.

"No way!" Amy objected. "It doesn't work like that. You never see older women with younger men—"

Jessica interrupted her in a loud voice. "Check this out, you two!" she called. "I've perfected the cheerleading jump you were having trouble with the other day!"

"What jump—" Amy began, but Lila just rolled her eyes and shook her head.

Jessica didn't care if Lila knew her true motives. She sprang into the air and executed a perfect no-hands cartwheel, landing in a split that couldn't help but impress the gorgeous guy.

The woman in red gestured to him, and he raised his camera again. Jessica obliged him by launching into a series of back springs. Ten yards away she saw Heather bound into the air with a Trojan crunch, followed by a perfect stag leap.

"Score one . . . for the Wakefield twin!" Jessica exclaimed, panting for breath. She gave Lila a high five as Chrome Dome led the pair away. "He took pictures of me instead of her! Did you see the look on Heather's face? I don't blame her for being mad after the way she pranced around in front of him!"

"I don't know," Lila said, peering after the departing group thoughtfully. "It looked to me as if he might have taken some shots of Heather too. Not to mention the rest of us. You do remember there were other people cheering here besides you and Her Horridness?"

"You think he took a shot of Heather?" Jessica asked anxiously. "I wish someone would take a shot *at* her!"

"You know," Amy reminded her, "Heather wasn't the only one prancing around for him."

"She's right, Jess," said Lila. "You couldn't have been more obvious if you'd spelled out Take Me, I'm Yours with your pom-poms!"

Jessica smirked at her. "You're just jealous because a cute boy saw you crouching in the mud. Get over it, Li!"

"Hey, having me come to this practice was your idea, not mine," Lila warned. "If you're going to abuse me . . ."

Jessica smiled warmly and placed an arm around her friend. "Sorry," she said. "You know how much I appreciate that you're taking Sara's place for a while."

"I still haven't agreed to fill in indefinitely!" Lila reminded her. "Our deal was just for practice today."

Sara Eastbourne was a talented dancer who'd

joined Jessica's upstart cheerleading squad. Like Jade and Patty, she'd had no cheering experience, but she'd worked hard and learned quickly. After nationals some of the girls had decided to leave the newly merged squad, but Sara had stuck with it.

Jessica thought the eight cheerleaders on the current squad brought an awesome mix of talent to the field: she and Heather the Horrible as cocaptains, backed by Sara, Amy, Patty, Maria, Annie, and Jade. But Sara had sprained her ankle. So Jessica was hoping that Lila would cover for Sara for a few weeks.

"Come on, Li," Jessica urged. "It'll be fun for us to cheer together again—just like old times. And you *are* one of the best cheerleaders around!"

"That goes without saying," Lila agreed. "But cheering is so unsophisticated."

Amy tossed her long, ash blond hair behind her shoulders. "Well, as much as I love being insulted like this, I need to talk to Jade and Patty about the new dance sequence they choreographed for the Get Excited cheer."

"Better do it now," Lila advised, "while Heather's busy bawling out Maria because her herkies aren't high enough."

Jessica nodded. "As soon as the Dragon Lady is done there she'll be back in our faces, throwing one of her temper tantrums about how she's the only one who works hard enough."

"Temper tantrums," Amy said with a sigh. "And

18

you said cheerleading was unsophisticated!"

As Amy skipped off to find Jade and Patty, Lila turned back to Jessica. "Why don't you ask your sister to take Sara's spot, Jess? I'm sure Elizabeth would be *thrilled* to help out her beloved twin." Lila smiled innocently, but Jessica knew sarcasm when she heard it.

"*As if!*" Jessica scoffed. Despite their identical heart-shaped faces, shoulder-length blond hair, and trim, athletic figures, the Wakefield twins had vastly different tastes when it came to after-school activities. Serious, sensitive Elizabeth hated cheerleading about as much as happy-go-lucky Jessica hated studying. Jessica's other favorite pastimes included scoping guys, dancing to the latest music, and shopping. Elizabeth would rather read a book, write an article for the school newspaper, the *Oracle,* or hang out with her cute—but insanely dull—boyfriend, Todd Wilkins, whom Elizabeth had been dating since the start of recorded history.

As soon as the cheerleading squad had returned with the second-place trophy from the national competition, Elizabeth had gladly handed over her uniform and vowed never to pick up a pom-pom again.

"You know Liz only joined the squad because I was desperate to show up Heather," Jessica reminded Lila.

"Right. And the fact that you *blackmailed* her had nothing to do with it?"

19

Jessica shrugged. "We all do what we have to do. I was up against the Dragon Lady, and I needed Liz. You of all people should see that I couldn't afford to be nice."

"True," Lila said. "There's no place for *nice* when it comes to business. You were defending your enterprise against Heather's hostile takeover."

"Speaking of nice, did you see the way that photographer's jeans fit him?" Jessica asked, gazing thoughtfully in the direction of the school. "Nothing gets much nicer than that! I think I'm in love."

Lila sighed wearily. "Is this the *third* time this month or the *fourth*, Jessica? You don't even know his name."

"What's in a name?" Jessica asked philosophically. She cocked her head. "Didn't somebody famous say that?"

"Probably someone with a name like Seymour or Maurice."

"Well, this guy's name isn't Seymour," Jessica declared. "He's much too cute to have a nerdy name."

"Whoever he is, did you see the way Heather's eyes latched onto him?" Lila asked.

Jessica laughed. "Like the look Winston Egbert gets when someone shows him a hamburger!" Tall, skinny Winston—Maria's boyfriend and the junior-class clown—had a legendary capacity for junk food.

20

"Heather *did* look ready to devour poor Seymour the Photographer. I bet she'll know his real name and vital statistics by the end of the day," Lila predicted, picking dried mud out from under her long, manicured fingernails.

"I wouldn't be surprised," Jessica said. "Even if Heather wasn't interested in him, she'd do whatever she could to keep him from liking me!" She folded her arms and lowered her eyebrows. "So I'm not going to let her. It's that easy."

"Jessica," Lila warned, "no schemes, please." She groaned. "I know that look on your face. Just leave me out of it, Wakefield."

"No scheme," Jessica said innocently, holding out her hands as if to show they were empty. "I just plan to find out who that drop-dead-gorgeous stranger is—before Heather does."

"Oh, yes?" Lila asked, her eyebrows impressively arched.

Jessica narrowed her eyes at Heather for a moment and then turned back to look at her best friend with a big smile on her face. "Yes," she replied. "Consider it a solemn vow."

Chapter 2

Elizabeth Wakefield rushed into the principal's office Wednesday afternoon, out of breath. The secretary was gone for the day, so Elizabeth knocked on the door of the inner office. "Mr. Cooper?" she called. But the door was ajar, and she could see that the room was empty. She'd been afraid she wouldn't be on time for her meeting with the principal. But *he* was the one who was late.

Elizabeth plopped herself into a chair in the waiting room. She checked her watch. It was four o'clock, exactly the time Mr. Cooper had asked her to stop by. She'd gotten caught up in an article she'd been writing in the *Oracle* office and had nearly lost track of the time.

Oh, well, she figured. *I might as well put the wait to good use*. She pulled the manuscript from her backpack and read through the first page once more. The article was about a new rule requiring each student activity to have a faculty adviser. *Like Mr. Collins,* she thought. The English teacher helped the newspaper staff with everything from designing a front page to getting along with their parents. He was more than a teacher and adviser—he was a friend and confidante.

Some students Elizabeth had talked to for her article were angry about the new requirement. "We don't need a baby-sitter!" the head of the prom committee had complained in an interview. But Elizabeth thought every student group should be lucky enough to have somebody like Mr. Collins.

In fact, the principal had said Mr. Collins would be at this meeting today. She'd tried to find the handsome English teacher earlier to ask what Mr. Cooper wanted to talk about. But the newspaper advisor hadn't been at the *Oracle* office that afternoon.

Elizabeth checked her watch again. The principal was ten minutes late. She was growing more and more curious about why he wanted to talk to her. She grinned. If she were Jessica, she'd have to assume she was in trouble for something, like failing an algebra exam or scamming her way out of history class. But Elizabeth was the responsible twin. When it came to trouble, her usual role was bailing Jessica out of it.

The principal would probably ask her to organize

a charity drive, tutor a struggling student, or write a press release for some school event. Or maybe he had a problem with an article that had run in the *Oracle*—after all, Mr. Collins was coming too.

No, if that was it, Penny would be here, she decided. Penny Ayala, a senior who was a close friend of Elizabeth's, was editor in chief of the school paper.

Mr. Cooper had said he wouldn't keep her long. Elizabeth wasn't worried. She and Jessica were supposed to ride home from school together in their Jeep Wrangler. But cheerleading practice wouldn't be over until four-thirty, and Jessica would probably hang out in the locker room long afterward, combing her hair, reapplying her makeup, and gabbing with her friends.

The outer door opened and the principal walked in, followed by Mr. Collins and two strangers. Elizabeth stuffed the newspaper article into her backpack and stood up to greet them.

As Elizabeth turned to introduce herself to the male visitor, she gasped.

She was staring up into the face of one of the best-looking guys she had ever seen!

Jessica, Lila, and Amy lagged behind the other girls walking toward the locker room after practice. Lila shoved her pom-poms at Jessica. "The least you can do is carry these filthy things for me," she said.

"They're not filthy!" Jessica protested. But she took the pom-poms. She hated letting Lila boss her around, but she needed her friend's cooperation.

"They were lying in the *dirt* while we made that ridiculous pyramid," Lila reminded her.

"You make dirt sound like toxic waste," Amy said.

"They weren't even in the dirt—they were lying on the grass," Jessica corrected. "And the pyramid isn't ridiculous. It's a total showstopper!"

"It was awesome," Amy agreed. "The crowd will go bananas when we do it at the soccer game this weekend!"

"*We?*" Lila asked.

"Oh, come on, Lila! Be on the squad with us," Jessica urged.

"You might as well give in right now, Lila," Amy said reasonably. "If you don't, Jessica will wheedle shamelessly until you do. It would save us all a lot of time if you just said yes now."

Jessica gave her a dirty look. "You're a big help."

"You've got to admit it was fun today," Amy said quickly to Lila.

Lila glowered. "I broke a nail today!" she complained. "And Bo is coming this weekend!"

"Horrors! Whatever will he say?" Amy mocked.

Jessica wanted to make a disparaging remark about Lila's snooty boyfriend, but she held her tongue. She needed her friend's cooperation, not her wrath. "I'll give you a manicure tonight, Lila," Jessica promised. "Just say you'll cheer with us until Sara's ankle is better. It's only for a week or so!"

"Well, maybe two or three weeks," Amy amended.

Jessica stopped walking and folded her tanned arms across the front of her tank top. She stared at Lila. "What is it now, Li?"

"What's what?" Lila asked, stopping short.

"You're having an expression."

Lila sighed. "I just don't know about being a cheerleader again, Jess. Look at what I had to do today: kneeling in the dirt? Face it, there was a major ick factor!"

"But you were awesome in the hip-hop cheer!" Jessica said. "And remember, Bo will be here for the soccer game. We'll be wearing the fancy uniforms you picked out for nationals, with the lace trim. You look sexier in those than anyone else!"

"Well, yes," Lila admitted. "But I left the squad for a reason! I'm just not into cheerleading the way you are, Jess."

"I left the squad for a long time too," Amy said. "But I'm back, and I'm sticking with it this time."

"Without you, Li, we've only got seven girls," Jessica said. "That's not enough to perform some of our best cheers! You know we need at least eight."

"The championship squad had twelve," Amy reminded them.

Lila shrugged. "And whose fault is it that you're down to eight?"

"What's that supposed to mean?" Jessica asked, stung. "*You're* the one who left! And we all knew Elizabeth would be toast as soon as nationals were over."

"But you have to admit, Jess, that Jean West and Sandy Bacon might have stayed if not for all the bickering between you and Heather," Amy said.

Jessica lowered her eyebrows menacingly. "I don't bicker with that two-faced brat. She's the one who does the bickering."

"Whatever," Amy said. "But it gets old fast."

"I don't know," Lila said. "Personally, I find the Jessica-and-Heather fireworks displays entertaining."

Amy rolled her eyes. "You would."

The three girls had stopped about twenty yards from the outside door to the locker room. The other cheerleaders had gone inside, but now Heather appeared at the doorway, her hands on her slender hips. "I know it's hard keeping up with the rest of us when you're out of shape!" she called out in a syrupy voice. "But you need to drag yourselves in here. We have business to discuss!"

Jessica smiled sweetly. "We wouldn't miss it, Heather! Why don't you hit the showers while you wait? I didn't want to say anything in front of the others, but you were looking way sweaty out there!"

Heather's eyes flashed. She opened her mouth to respond but shut it with an exasperated shake of her golden mane. Then she turned around and stomped back inside, the door swinging shut behind her.

Jessica chuckled. "I think eight is the perfect number for our squad," she said. "But it would be more perfect if one of the eight wasn't Heather the Horrible!"

"And you want me to put up with that brat just to do you a favor?" Lila asked.

"Even with Heather around," Amy told Lila, "you've got to admit it's a total trip, being part of the squad that won second place in the whole country!"

"I can't argue with fame and admiration," Lila conceded.

"It'll be especially fun for the three of us to be famous and admired together," Jessica said. "After all, we are the Three Musketeers!" She grinned mischievously. "Make that the Three Muske-cheers!"

Lila tried to hide a smile. "OK, OK, I'll fill in until Sara's back," she agreed finally. "But this is not because I'm doing anyone any favors!"

"Of course not," Jessica said, shaking her head solemnly. "You wouldn't want to ruin your hard-earned reputation."

"The truth is that I need the exercise," Lila admitted. "My personal trainer, Hugo, just ran off for an extended vacation in Switzerland—"

Jessica sighed dramatically. "It is so hard to get good help nowadays."

"And the latest runway shows are all featuring clingy knits!" Lila said. "I can't afford to lose muscle tone while Hugo's in the Alps."

"Good point," Jessica said seriously.

"But remember," Lila continued, "this is only until Sara's ankle is better. There are limits, you know, even for best friends. *Especially* for best friends!"

"I apologize for being late, Elizabeth," Mr. Cooper said. "I was taking our visitors on a tour of the school and grounds before we moved on to Mr. Collins's office. I'm afraid we got a bit behind schedule."

"No problem, Mr. Cooper," Elizabeth said, wrenching her eyes away from the tall, brown-haired stranger who stood beside the principal, a camera hanging from his neck. "I used the extra time to work on a story for the *Oracle*."

Mr. Cooper beamed. "That is exactly what I meant about this young lady," he said to the two visitors. Standing beside the attractive young man was a slender blond woman in a red Chanel suit. "Elizabeth is one of our most dedicated and hard-working students," Mr. Cooper concluded.

"Diane and Brad," Mr. Collins said, gesturing toward the two visitors after the principal ushered

29

the group into his office, "this is Elizabeth Wakefield, the student journalist we told you about. Liz, our visitors are from *Scoop* magazine. This is Diane Norton, a senior writer, and Brad Cotter, a photographer—"

Before he could continue, the tall, glamorous woman reached out and shook Elizabeth's hand. "Call me Diane, please. And this is Brad, *assistant* photographer."

Elizabeth noticed she emphasized the word *assistant*. Brad just grinned and stuck out his hand.

"You're familiar with *Scoop*?" Diane asked.

"Yes, of course," Elizabeth said, taking a seat in Mr. Cooper's office. *Scoop* was a hip, quirky national magazine with a growing reputation. "It's a weekly, one of the hottest publications around! But isn't it put out by CCB Media Group, in New York? What brings you to the West Coast? A story?"

"That's right," Diane said. "I'm writing an article on the Girls of Seventy-six."

"That was the first Sweet Valley High cheerleading squad ever to go to the national championship," Mr. Collins supplied.

"I thought *we* were the first," Elizabeth said, puzzled.

Mr. Cooper nodded, leaning forward across his desk. "I'm afraid I may have perpetrated that myth myself when I was praising this year's squad," he admitted. "The truth is, I simply didn't know about

30

the 1976 squad. After all, that was long before I came to Sweet Valley."

"Our state trophy was stolen from the display case a few weeks after nationals," Diane explained. "As far as I know, it was never recovered, but we didn't mind. We knew we were the best cheerleading squad in California!"

"We?" Elizabeth asked. "You mean *you* were on that cheerleading squad?"

Diane smiled. "Yes, I was a senior here in 1976. We didn't place at nationals, like this year's squad did. But winning the state championship—and just being at the national competition—was the highlight of my high-school career!"

"But you know all about that," Brad said to Elizabeth. He was friendly enough, and he had a very sexy smile, but she didn't like the way he kept staring at her. "Mr. Collins tells us you're not only a writer but also part of the Sweet Valley cheerleading squad that went to nationals this year and took second place!"

"I was there, all right," Elizabeth agreed. "And you're right, Diane—it was an amazing experience. But I've got to tell you, my heart isn't in cheerleading. More than anything I want to be a writer."

"You're an awfully good cheerleader for someone whose heart isn't in it," Brad said.

Elizabeth was confused for a moment. The photographer spoke as if he'd seen her cheer, but he couldn't have been at nationals. Then she remembered that the cheerleading association had videotaped the final stage of the competition. He and Diane must have watched the tapes to prepare for their story.

She opened her mouth to tell them she was no longer on the cheerleading squad, but the principal spoke first. "Elizabeth is one of the most multi-talented students at Sweet Valley High," Mr. Cooper said. He rose to his feet and walked around to the front of his desk. "We're all proud of her accomplishments."

Elizabeth felt herself blushing. Mr. Cooper always made her uncomfortable when he treated her like a show-and-tell exhibit. She knew he was eager to put Sweet Valley High's best foot forward with visitors. And it was flattering that he thought she was one of the most accomplished students in the whole school. But it was also embarrassing and a lot to live up to.

Mr. Collins winked at her behind the principal's back, and Elizabeth felt a rush of gratitude.

"Elizabeth, we'd like you to help us with this story," Diane said. "My family moved away from California right after graduation. I went to college at Columbia, and I've been in New York City ever since. I need someone who lives in Sweet Valley— someone who knows the school, the town, and the people—to help research this article."

"Mr. Collins said you were the best person for the job," Brad said in a slow, easy voice. "And it

32

looks like he's right—a cheerleader and a student journalist. We couldn't do better!"

"What's the focus of the story?" Elizabeth asked.

"We're calling it 'The Girls of Seventy-six: Where Are They Now?'" Diane replied.

"Every month we do a different 'Where Are They Now?' feature," Brad explained. "Sometimes we do famous people, like child actors. But most of the time it's just someone who once did something interesting or offbeat—something people can relate to."

"My editor found out I was on a championship cheerleading squad from a school that placed in this year's competition," Diane said. "And she thought it would make a great story."

"It is a great idea," Elizabeth said, trying to keep the excitement out of her voice in order to maintain a sense of professionalism. "What do you need me to do?"

"We've got current addresses for three of the girls from my squad," Diane said. "And me, of course. That leaves four former cheerleaders we still need to locate. Do you think you can help us?"

"Liz, if your work is useful, Diane tells me she can give you a credit in the magazine for research assistance," Mr. Collins said. "It would be a wonderful opportunity for you, and I can help smooth the way with your other teachers if the time commitment is a problem."

Elizabeth's heart was racing so fast, she could hardly breathe. Her work—maybe even her name—in *Scoop* magazine! It would be at every newsstand and magazine store in America. She couldn't wait to tell Jessica. And her boyfriend, Todd Wilkins.

"Yes, I'd love to!" she said finally. "In fact, I can start right away. I've still got some time this evening before I need to leave school. I'll head straight to the library when we're finished here and look up some old yearbooks."

Elizabeth could hardly wait to get started!

"Jessica Wakefield, you are the most immature person I've ever met," Heather said in an exasperated voice as the cheerleaders sat on benches in the locker room.

"Don't think of it as immature," Jessica urged. "Think of it as *flexible*."

"But it's already four-thirty!"

"Wow! Did everyone hear that?" Jessica asked the others. "Heather learned how to tell time!"

"You are such a nimrod."

"And you're a control freak!"

"Can we get on with it, you two?" Maria asked. "We were supposed to be out of here at four-thirty. And we haven't even started our business meeting."

"That's just what I was trying to do," Heather said. "If Jessica will stop giving me attitude and keep her mouth shut!"

34

"Why should *you* run the meeting? I'm a co-captain too. And I was here long before you ever heard of Sweet Valley!"

"Fine, Jessica. You start the meeting," Heather said sweetly. "But you don't even know what we need to discuss."

"As always, I have my own agenda," Jessica told her. "First I want to announce that Lila has agreed to be on the squad for the next few weeks, until Sara's ankle is healed."

"Way to go, Lila!" Jade cheered. "That's great. Seven is a lousy number to try to choreograph a routine for."

"And you just decided this, Jessica, without consulting me?" Heather asked.

Lila raised her chin and looked down her nose at Heather. "Do you have a problem with it?"

Heather shrugged. "Not with you, Lila. We're glad to have you back on the squad. It's just the way the decision was made—"

"I have every right to—" Jessica interrupted.

"Honestly, will you two chill out?" Patty pleaded. "You're driving the rest of us wiggy with this constant picking at each other! Can you put a lid on it for a half hour, at least?"

"I second that motion," Maria said in a formal tone of voice, rising from the bench. "And now, to keep Jess and Heather from scratching each other's eyes out, *I* am officially taking over this meeting!"

"You can't do—" Heather began, but Maria silenced her with a glare.

"First of all, I think I speak for everyone else when I say welcome back, Lila!" Maria said. "But there is some real business we need to discuss, and I'm the one who was going to announce it anyhow. So I might as well run the show. Any objections?"

She stared pointedly at Heather, who shook her head. Then she turned to Jessica.

Maria's father was the town mayor, but Jessica had never heard the petite brunette sound so authoritative. She sighed. Maria and the others were probably right to be annoyed with their cocaptains. The Pom-pom Wars were supposed to be over, but the Cold War between Jessica and Heather was a drain on everyone.

"No objections here either," Jessica said sincerely. "And I'm sorry. I didn't mean to let my personal feelings get in the way of things. You all know how much this squad means to me. I wouldn't want anything to come between all of us."

Heather bestowed one of her sugary smiles on Jessica. "I'm sorry too. Go on, Maria. Tell us your news."

"As student council vice president, I'm supposed to talk to you about the new requirement that all student activities have a faculty adviser," Maria said, pulling a clipboard out of her gym bag.

Jessica felt a wave of foreboding. "I have an overwhelming sense of ickiness about this."

"We've all heard rumors about the faculty adviser rule," Patty said. "But what does it have to do with us? I thought it applied only to clubs. Cheerleading's more of a sport, isn't it?"

Maria shrugged. "Yes, but when you think about it, the other varsity sports have faculty advisers already—their coaches." She read from a memo on her clipboard. "'The new rule applies to all student groups whose activities take place on school property or who present themselves as official representatives of Sweet Valley High.'"

"The art club has always had Ms. Markey, the art teacher, as an adviser," Jade pointed out. "David says she's a big help to them." Her boyfriend, David Prentiss, was one of the most talented painters at school. "And Ms. Dalton sponsors the French club and that works out OK. What's the big deal?"

"Are you kidding? It *reeks!*" Jessica complained. "Why do cheerleaders need a faculty adviser?"

"Because the school board passed a rule," Maria answered. "Look, girls. The requirement is not up for debate. Student council didn't like it any better than you do, but we don't have a choice. Come on, it won't be so bad if we get somebody we like!"

"So who are they sticking us with?" Annie asked. "I can't think of a single teacher I'd want to have watching us practice our routines."

"Except Mr. Collins, maybe," Amy said. "At least he's cute."

"No way!" Jessica objected. "He's one of those I-want-to-be-your-friend types. He'd be in our faces all the time. Besides, he's already busy with the *Oracle* after school."

"I know I agreed to be on the squad for a while," Lila said. "But I didn't know that meant hanging out with *teachers* after the school day's over. That's harsh!"

"It doesn't even have to be a teacher," Maria said, peering down at her clipboard. "Any staff member can be an adviser, providing Mr. Cooper approves the choice. Guidance counselors, administrators, teachers' aides . . ."

"How about the janitor?" Jessica suggested archly. "Or the guy who fixes the furnace?"

Heather stood up from where she'd been sitting on one of the locker-room benches. "This is terrible!" she cried. "None of the staff members knows a thing about cheerleading! *We're a championship squad.* And they want us to risk the quality of our performances by letting some athletically challenged dictator call the shots?"

"Bummer!" Jessica exclaimed with feeling. "I don't want some faculty member telling us what to do!" *It's bad enough having Heather telling us what to do,* she added silently.

"The good news is we can choose our own adviser," Maria said. "We've got until Friday to talk somebody into doing it. If we don't have an adviser by then, Mr. Cooper will assign someone."

"That would be fatal," Jessica said glumly.

"How can we stand for this?" Heather asked, waving her arms at the other cheerleaders. "Think about it. We've been talking about jazzing up our act even more: sexier cheers, more modern music, more daring maneuvers. . . ."

"How can we do all that with a teacher hanging around, worrying about whether our skirts are too short or our moves are too dangerous?" Jessica asked. For once she was in total agreement with her cocaptain.

"I guess you're right," Jade conceded. "We'll lose a lot of artistic freedom if we have to answer to a teacher about everything we want to do."

"An adviser will cramp our style," Lila added.

Heather turned slowly and stared at them all, one by one. "Then we'll just have to find an adviser who won't give us any trouble," she said, steely determination in her voice.

Jessica jumped to her feet. "Heather is absolutely right!" she said, though the words tasted bitter in her mouth. She still despised her cocaptain, but her beloved cheerleaders were in danger. She and Heather would have to work together to save the squad.

Chapter 3

After the meeting in Mr. Cooper's office, Elizabeth walked through the empty corridor to the school library.

"Elizabeth, wait up!" called a voice behind her. She turned to see Brad sauntering toward her. "I was hoping I could catch you."

"Was there something else you needed my help with for the story?" Elizabeth asked.

"I don't know about the story," Brad said, "but I really could use your help. I've never even been on the West Coast before, let alone in Sweet Valley. I don't know a soul here except for you."

Once again he was staring at Elizabeth in a way that made her uncomfortable—as if he could see through her white blouse and slim-cut navy skirt. She continued walking down the hallway, keeping her eyes ahead of her. Brad fell in beside her. "Do you, uh, need directions to someplace?" she asked.

"Directions to the nearest party!" Brad replied. "I've got to go with Diane to interview the basketball coach in a few minutes. But later this evening, how about you showing me some of the local nightlife? You look like the kind of girl who's always up for a party!"

"I haven't heard of any parties tonight," Elizabeth said quickly. She didn't want to be rude to Brad since they'd be working together on the cheerleader story. But she didn't want to encourage any potential advances either.

"Then we'll create our own!" Brad said. "I've hosted some of the most radical bashes in New York City, Liz. My father has the use of this amazing corporate penthouse. . . . Did I mention that he's Lawrence Cotter, the first *C* in CCB Media Group?"

"Uh, no," Elizabeth said. "You didn't. That's the same CCB that owns *Scoop*?"

"The one and only," Brad bragged. "When I decided to take a few years off before college, Dad insisted that I get a job, starting at the bottom. That's how I ended up at *Scoop*."

"There's nothing like having connections," Elizabeth said.

"Nepotism—the game the whole family can play!" Brad shot back flippantly.

Ugh! Elizabeth thought. *He actually seems proud of the fact that he got his job only because*

41

his father's the boss. Even more amazing was the fact that he expected *her* to be impressed by it!

"Speaking of games," Brad said, placing an arm around her shoulders, "why don't we get together tonight and play a few, one-on-one? You can show me where all the cool people hang out in this town."

Elizabeth dodged his arm. "Sorry, Brad, but I have a steady boyfriend."

"That didn't keep you from noticing me out on the football field an hour or two back," he replied smoothly. "When I was shooting the cheerleaders."

Shooting the cheerleaders?

For a moment Elizabeth was alarmed. Then she realized he meant shooting them with his camera. Suddenly his attitude made sense. From the very beginning he'd mistaken her for Jessica, who must have been showing off for the good-looking stranger during cheerleading practice.

"That wasn't me noticing you," she said wryly.

"You're playing hard to get," he accused. "But it's not going to work. You don't expect me to believe there's someone else around school who looks just like you!"

"Actually, I do," Elizabeth replied, stopping at the door to the school library. "Bye, Brad. I have some research to do now. I'll talk to you tomorrow. *About the story,*" she added pointedly.

Soft rock music spilled from the library door as Elizabeth pulled it open. She slipped inside and closed the door firmly behind her, leaving Brad standing in the hall.

Lila sighed impatiently. So far the cheerleaders hadn't come up with the name of a single staff member who'd make a good adviser. The more they talked as they changed their clothes and gathered their books together Wednesday afternoon, the more relieved Lila felt that she was on the squad only temporarily.

"What about Ms. Dalton?" Jade asked. "She's nice, and she seems fairly athletic. French club only meets once a month, so that wouldn't cause a conflict."

"Over my dead body!" said Amy, folding a towel into her duffel bag. "That woman hates me! You should see the kind of grades she gives me."

"I thought she gave you bad grades because you're rotten at French," Lila pointed out as she rooted through Jessica's backpack to borrow a hairbrush.

"Well, that too," Amy admitted. "But I still think she hates me."

Jessica laughed. "I can see it now. The Sweet Valley cheerleaders take to the field to cheer on the Gladiators. Except Ms. Dalton makes us do it entirely in French!"

"What's French for 'Go, Gladiators'?" Annie asked with a giggle.

"Search me," Amy replied. "All I know about

speaking French is that you're supposed to sound as if you've got a golf ball in your mouth."

Heather shook her head. "Then Dalton's out. We need to smile when we cheer!"

"I've got it!" Patty exclaimed suddenly. She paused until they were all listening. "Mr. Russo, the chemistry teacher!"

Maria shrieked with laughter. "Have you noticed him sitting in the stands at soccer games? He goes ballistic every time a player misses a goal! The poor guy would have a heart attack before he's forty if he had to watch every game for every sport."

"Could you imagine choreographing a pyramid with Mr. Frankel, my math teacher?" Jade asked. "We'd be calculating the trajectory of every dismount!"

"Whatever that means," said Amy, rolling her eyes.

"I say we ask Mrs. Waller," Jessica suggested glibly.

"The school dietitian?" Annie asked.

Jessica stood up, grabbed the nearest pair of pom-poms, and improvised a cheer:

Hamburgers, pizza, mystery meat!
Sweet Valley Gladiators can't be beat!
Overcooked spinach, undercooked peas,
We're the team that aims to please!

°　　°　　°

Jade was giggling so hard, she fell against her locker. "I hate to break up this creative brainstorming session, but I have to get going. It was hard enough convincing my parents to let me become a cheerleader in the first place. If I'm late for dinner, they'll ground me!"

"I'm glad my parents aren't that strict!" Lila said. She truly felt sorry for the delicately pretty sophomore. Sometimes she wished her own parents had more time for her, but family togetherness was desirable only up to a point. Jade's parents, in Lila's opinion, were way too overprotective.

"Me too!" Jessica said. "But then there's my sister, Ms. Punctuality. And she's got the keys to the Jeep. What time is it anyway?"

"Five o'clock," Patty said.

"Weren't you supposed to meet Elizabeth fifteen minutes ago?" Lila asked Jessica.

"If Liz has left you stranded," Annie said, "I'd be happy to give you a lift. I've got Mom's Escort today, and I'm leaving in just a minute." Annie's family lived near the Wakefields on Calico Drive.

"Thanks, but I don't think I need it. Liz wouldn't go home without me."

"I could use a ride, Annie," Amy said.

"Sure thing," said Annie. "Are you sure we're not leaving you stranded, Jess?"

"Liz knows I'm in here. I bet she got tied up in some deadly dull assignment for the *Oracle,* covering a chess club tournament or something.

45

You know she loves that kind of stuff."

Lila rolled her eyes. "Your sister is *so* uncool. I would be mortified to be related to someone like that."

"Oh, she's OK," Jessica said. "She's definitely useful to have around when I need to borrow money or clothes."

"Or her identity," Lila added. The twins were famous for pretending to be each other, especially when Jessica had something to gain from pulling a switch.

"Whatever works," Jessica said with a grin. "Anyhow, she'll come looking for me if she needs me. In the meantime, I need to take a shower before I go home. Are you leaving, Li?"

"Yes, I am *out of here*," Lila said. "Call me tonight, Jessica."

"And everyone think hard about who we can get as our cheerleading adviser," Maria reminded them as most of the girls started heading for the door. "We'll talk about it again tomorrow."

Jim Croce was singing "Time in a Bottle" on the stereo as Elizabeth walked into the library at five o'clock that evening. A woman with long, light brown hair was standing at the reference desk. Her back was to the door, but Elizabeth recognized her right away.

"Hi, Ms. Swanson!" she called to the assistant librarian, practically skipping into the room in her haste to leave Brad behind and get started on her research for *Scoop*.

Nancy Swanson turned and smiled shyly. "Hello, Elizabeth," she greeted in a tentative voice. "It's always nice to see you here. I can turn off the music if it bothers you. Technically I'm not supposed to be playing it in here, but officially the library's closed for the evening."

"Oh, I'm sorry!" Elizabeth said. "Do you want me to leave? I can come back tomorrow."

"No, of course not," Ms. Swanson replied. "I have another half hour of work to do. There's no reason why you can't look around."

"Thanks," Elizabeth said. "And don't turn off your music. I always thought this was a pretty song. I just wanted to get a head start on some research tonight while Jessica's finishing up with the cheerleaders. I only need a few minutes." Elizabeth had run into Annie at her locker and learned that Jessica was still taking a shower, so she figured she had time to glance through a few yearbooks at least.

"How are you doing, Liz?" Ms. Swanson asked. "And how is your sister? The cheerleaders looked *far out* at the field hockey game last weekend! It's too bad Sara hurt her ankle."

"I missed the game," Elizabeth admitted. "But I agree about Sara. Besides that, though, Jessica was psyched about the cheerleaders' performance. She's been raving about it for days."

47

"The crowd really dug them."

Elizabeth looked at her curiously. "You never miss a game, do you? Of any sport! Not many faculty members make that much of an effort to show some school spirit. I don't even know many students who do!"

"I just like to support my school," the assistant librarian replied, raising a hand to her face as if to hide her expression.

As always, Elizabeth felt sorry for the woman. Nancy Swanson had been working at Sweet Valley High for only a few months, but she'd always been extraordinarily attentive to the students, especially the most popular ones. She always seemed to hang on Elizabeth's every word. And she never failed to ask about Jessica, though Elizabeth was sure her sister hadn't been in the library more than two or three times during her entire high-school career.

"Can I help you find anything today?" the assistant librarian asked.

"No, I think I know where to find what I need," Elizabeth replied. Suddenly she realized what Ms. Swanson reminded her of. She was like one of those insecure teenagers who was always trying too hard to fit in and who never succeeded precisely because she tried too hard.

For instance, Ms. Swanson dressed in the retro, seventies styles that the fashion magazines said were "in" among high-school kids. But she overdid it. Even the most stylish of teenagers didn't wear hip huggers, color-blocked dresses, or embroidered gauze tops every single day. Today Ms. Swanson had on a pair of close-fitting, low-rise pants in a herringbone pattern under a shiny polyester blouse and a fringed vest. To complete the image, she even peppered her language with seventies slang. She obviously hadn't noticed that nobody used phrases like "dig it" and "far out" anymore, not even the most retro-dressed students.

There was definitely something odd about the bland, quiet assistant librarian, Elizabeth thought. The woman always had a lonely, vaguely wistful look in her bright blue eyes. But Elizabeth couldn't fault someone who was always so friendly and eager to please.

"What's your research for?" asked Ms. Swanson. "That poetry paper for Mr. Collins's class?"

"You're really amazing," Elizabeth said. "I don't know how you keep track of what every teacher has assigned, but you always know!"

Ms. Swanson covered her mouth with her hand again. Elizabeth knew it was a common habit of people who were extremely timid and easily embarrassed. Elizabeth felt sorry for her. She smiled encouragingly, ignoring the woman's blush.

"Actually my poetry paper is under control," Elizabeth said. "But maybe you can help with the research I need to do for another project." If there was one thing Ms. Swanson was good at, it was her job.

Maybe she'd feel better if she could help Elizabeth. "I'm working with a reporter from *Scoop* magazine, researching a story she's writing about Sweet Valley High. It's about the Girls of Seventy-six."

The assistant librarian's blush grew deeper. One corner of her mouth seemed to twitch downward, and she covered her lips with her hand again. "The Girls of Seventy-six?" she asked in a faraway voice.

"Don't feel bad," Elizabeth said with a smile. "I didn't know about them either. They were a Sweet Valley High cheerleading squad that won the 1976 state championship. The magazine is doing a piece on what they're all doing now. I need to look through some old yearbooks for background information."

"Nineteen seventy-six," Ms. Swanson repeated in her quiet voice. "That was a long time ago, wasn't it?" She paused for a moment and then gave Elizabeth a soft smile. "But you girls are a championship squad again this year! You know, Elizabeth, I'm surprised you decided not to stick with it. A lot of girls would give their right arms to be cheerleaders."

Elizabeth chuckled. "It might be hard to do the cheers without a right arm!" she joked. "Seriously, I'm just not a born cheerleader, like Jessica is. I can do the moves, but I always feel self-conscious out there in front of everyone. Besides, it feels like a waste of time. There are too many other things I want to be doing."

"School spirit is never a waste of time," Ms. Swanson said fervently.

"I hope a lot of other staff members feel that way," Elizabeth said. "Or this new faculty adviser rule is going to go down the tubes!"

"Have the cheerleaders picked an adviser yet?" Ms. Swanson asked, leading her into the stacks and pointing down the aisle to the section of bookshelves that contained the yearbooks.

"I don't think they've decided on anyone," Elizabeth replied. "Maria told me she was going to talk to the others this afternoon about choosing. It'll probably take them a few days to come up with a name. Then they'll need to convince that person to do it."

"I'm sure they won't have any trouble finding somebody. After all, this is a championship squad!"

Suddenly Elizabeth had a terrific idea. Nancy Swanson was full of school spirit, and she had a deep interest in cheerleading and team sports. If she became the cheerleading adviser, it might help her feel as if she was finally fitting into life at Sweet Valley High.

She smiled back at the assistant librarian for a second and then hurried to the yearbooks. But as she scanned the titles on the shelves, her mind wasn't on the Girls of '76. She was thinking about poor Ms. Swanson. Elizabeth felt suddenly full of determination to see the timid woman as cheerleading adviser.

"Now I just have to convince Jessica," she muttered under her breath.

Nancy Swanson watched Elizabeth's back as the girl walked farther into the stacks. Elizabeth had it all. She was bright, beautiful, and popular. Her sister was the flashy, exuberant Jessica. Her best friends were sweet, loyal Enid Rollins and sophisticated Maria Slater, a former child actress. And Elizabeth's boyfriend was Todd Wilkins, a basketball star and one of the best-looking boys at school. Teachers loved Elizabeth, and students looked up to her. Some people had everything.

"The Girls of Seventy-six," the assistant librarian repeated again under her breath. She could hardly believe she'd heard Elizabeth right. A familiar pain, a pinching sensation, gripped the left side of her face. The muscles tugged downward, pulling out of her control. Out of habit she covered her mouth with her hand. Suddenly she felt as if she were boiling over with hurt and anger.

"Why?" she whispered to herself. "It's not fair!"

Ms. Swanson scooted out of the rows of shelves until Elizabeth was out of sight. Then she closed her eyes and leaned against a bookcase until she regained control of her emotions.

Her hands balled into fists at her sides, and she told herself to let it go. She had to stay mellow. She couldn't start thinking about . . . *that* again.

It was too risky.

Chapter 4

Jessica stood at her locker, trying to decide if there was any point in bringing her poetry anthology home. Sure, she had a paper to write for Mr. Collins's class. But the paper wasn't due until Friday. And the book was obnoxiously heavy.

"Nah, who needs it?" she decided at last. Besides, she wouldn't have time to read poetry that night. She and Elizabeth were going out for pizza since their parents were having dinner with a client of Mrs. Wakefield's interior-design firm. After that, Jessica figured she'd be on the phone for hours with Lila and Amy and the other girls, trying to think of a teacher who wouldn't be a complete washout as a cheerleading adviser. Her English paper would have to wait. She had more pressing issues to worry about.

As Jessica took a step backward to swing the

metal locker door shut, she bumped into someone who must have just walked up behind her. Jessica jumped. She spun around, ready to give whoever it was a piece of her mind for sneaking up on her like that.

"I thought you were going to the library," said a smooth, sexy voice.

Jessica felt her eyebrows shoot halfway up her forehead. It was the gorgeous photographer from cheerleading practice! She basked in his wide grin, grateful for her last-minute decision to take a shower before leaving the locker room.

Suddenly his words registered. "Me, at the library? *Right.* And then they're going to elect me president of the chess club." She rolled her eyes. "Get a clue!"

He laughed. "I guess that means there really are two of you!"

"Let me guess," Jessica said, suddenly understanding. "You met my twin sister, Elizabeth. You say she's in the library? How boringly predictable."

"I saw her go through the door myself," he said. "Not exactly a party animal, is she?"

"Animal? Not unless it's Bambi," Jessica explained. "Liz is the quiet, wholesome type. But thanks for the tip. She's supposed to drive me home."

"*Now* I understand why I thought she was the girl I saw on the football field. You two really do look alike!" His eyes ran up and down her in a way

54

that made Jessica's entire body tingle appreciatively. "Oops, I guess I forgot to introduce myself.
I'm Brad Cotter. And I take it you're a Wakefield."

"Jessica," she said. "One half of the world-
famous Wakefield twins."

"The *amazingly identical* Wakefield twins," he
said with a whistle. "No wonder I mistook your
sister for you!"

Jessica felt her annoyance rising. She hated being
confused with Elizabeth—unless she was *trying* to
be confused with her, of course.

"Now that I've taken a better look," Brad continued, gazing into her eyes, "I'll revise my original
judgment. You two look a lot alike, but there *is* one
difference. Elizabeth is pretty. But you are definitely
more beautiful than she is."

That's much better, Jessica decided.

"And it sounds like you know a lot more than
your sister does about having a good time. Does
she always get her kicks in the library?"

"What can I say?" Jessica replied, throwing up
her hands. "I keep warning her that reading gives
you wrinkles, but Liz can be a megadrone. She's
the one to go to if you need someone to explain
subject-verb agreement or geometric proofs. But if
you want advice on where to have fun in Sweet
Valley, I'm your twin!"

"I like the sound of that," Brad murmured. He
touched her on the arm, and warmth spread
through Jessica's body, radiating outward from his

fingertips. "I bet you're wondering what I was doing out on the football sidelines today," he said.

Jessica nodded. "Now that you mention it . . . ," she began. "I mean, you don't strike me as the kind of guy who'd be all buddy-buddy with Chrome Dome Cooper."

Brad laughed. "I'm an assistant photographer with *Scoop* magazine," he explained. "The woman you saw with me is Diane Norton, a writer for the magazine. We're in town doing a story on the Sweet Valley High cheerleading squad of 1976."

Jessica raised her eyebrows. "Isn't that, like, ancient history?"

"It's one of those where-are-they-now things," he explained. Brad went on to tell her about the Girls of '76, and Jessica's hopes soared with every word.

"What about the current championship squad?" Jessica asked. "You'll want to include something about us, won't you?"

Brad nodded. "After seeing you in action today, I plan to push for a photograph as well as copy about you girls."

"Will that writer Ms. Norton go for it?"

"I think so. It's the hook that got the managing editor interested in the story in the first place—the whole now-and-then idea. Of course, the main focus will be on the Girls of Seventy-six and where they are now."

"Cool!" Jessica exclaimed. In her mind she could see a photograph of herself in *Scoop,* sticking her dismount perfectly. In the background most of the other cheerleaders still formed their human pyramid. But Heather . . . well, Heather had been cropped right out of the picture. *There just isn't enough room on the page for both of us!*

Of course, Jessica told herself, having her photograph in a national magazine in stores across the country would attract serious attention. After all, Paula Abdul had started as a cheerleader. Maybe a modeling agency scout would see her, or a talent agent. Then she'd have fame, fortune, and exciting modeling jobs. Her picture would be on the cover of *Ingenue,* then *Fashion Forward.* She might even appear on *Sports Illustrated* in a few years, wearing the world's sexiest bathing suit. Rhomboid, the rock group, would ask her to star in their new music video. Steven Spielberg would call with a movie offer. She'd be rich and famous, and Heather would be . . .

Walking toward me right now, Jessica realized, snapping out of her daydream. Sure enough, the slender blonde was strolling down the corridor toward Jessica and Brad, her hips swaying in an exaggerated version of her usual walk.

The most depressing part, Jessica thought, *is that Heather looks darn good.* Her white-blond curls bounced against her shoulders as she walked. She'd changed clothes since cheerleading practice, and her body-hugging white minidress set off her golden tan.

It's too bad Brad can't see those insectlike gossip

antennae poking out of her head, Jessica thought. Looking at Heather now, she was sure those antennae were targeted straight at the handsome photographer.

"You must be the photographer from *Scoop* magazine," Heather said in her most syrupy voice. She playfully took Brad's arm and wrapped both of her own arms around it. "My name is Heather Mallone, and I'm the head cheerleader here—the only person on the squad who'd been to nationals before this year. I went with my old school, you know, when I lived in Nevada."

Brad nodded. "I saw you practicing before. You're very good."

Heather smiled triumphantly. "I've been hearing so much about you, Brad!" she purred, stroking his arm. "Your upcoming story about the cheerleading squad has me totally psyched!"

"News travels fast," Jessica remarked in an acid tone.

"I do like photographers," Heather said, not even glancing at Jessica. "They know how to see the real beauty around them."

"It's not hard if you know where to look," Brad replied. Jessica's heart did a triple herky. He was staring straight at her! Unfortunately Heather didn't seem to notice.

"You know, Brad, since you're new in town and all, you probably need someone to introduce you to all the best places. Why don't I take you to the Dairi Burger right now! It's where all the important people from school hang out."

Brad smiled easily, but Jessica was sure his smile was sexier when he was looking at her, not at Heather. "Sorry, Heather, but I'm meeting with the basketball coach"—he checked his watch and bit his lip comically—"five minutes ago!"

"Then how about some other time?" Heather asked. "I'll give you the complete tour of Sweet Valley."

"Thanks for the offer, but I already accepted a promise of a tour from Jessica."

Jessica stared smugly at Heather, who pretended not to notice.

"Right now," the photographer continued, "I'm afraid I have to say farewell to both of you and head over to the gym. Nice to meet you, Heather. And Jessica, I'll see you around!"

"Sure thing, Brad!" Jessica called, reveling in the frozen smile on Heather's face. "And let me know when you're ready for me to show you around town!"

Jessica watched Brad's tight-fitting jeans as he sauntered away. After he turned the corner and was out of sight, she glanced at her cocaptain.

Heather was positively seething.

Elizabeth steered the Jeep through rush-hour traffic, trying to tune out Jessica's chatter so she could focus on her driving.

"You're not even listening to me!" Jessica complained.

"Well, I'm *trying* not to," Elizabeth said. "But I can't help myself!"

"Because I'm so entertaining?"

"Because you're so *loud*," Elizabeth explained. "You've been gabbing nonstop about Brad Cotter since the moment we got into the car. I don't see what the big deal is."

"Isn't it a blinding flash of the obvious?" Jessica asked. "The guy is drop-dead gorgeous! And you're going to be working with him! You could at least have the sense to gloat a little. That's what I would do."

"I could gloat about working for *Scoop*," Elizabeth admitted. "But not about working with Brad. He makes my skin crawl!"

"He can crawl on my skin anytime he wants," Jessica said with a smirk.

It figures, Elizabeth thought. Jessica had a history of being attracted to the wrong kind of guy. But the more Elizabeth objected, the more insistent Jessica would get about him. So she chose her words carefully. "He doesn't seem like a very nice person," Elizabeth said finally.

"I should hope not!" Jessica replied. "*Nice* is fine if you're looking for a long-term relationship—especially if you're a boring person like you, Liz."

"I am not—" Elizabeth protested.

"But this guy lives more than three thousand miles away," Jessica continued, speaking over her.

"He's going to be in town—what, a week? Two at the most, if Diane Norton can stretch out her business trip long enough to look up her old buddies. That makes Brad prime *fling* material, not relationship material. And *nice* is the kiss of death for a fling!"

"There's nothing wrong with *nice*," Elizabeth insisted. "Todd is a nice boy."

Jessica rolled her eyes. "I rest my case. Off the basketball court your boyfriend is the world's most boring hunk! Brad is a hunk too, but he knows how to have fun!"

"He sounds sleazy to me," Elizabeth said grumpily.

Jessica flashed her a big grin. "Sleazy is fun!"

"You're impossible," Elizabeth said.

"And you're always saying I shouldn't judge people unfairly. You've had what? Two conversations with the guy? Short conversations. But you've already decided he's scum."

"OK, I may have jumped to conclusions," Elizabeth admitted. "Maybe he was acting sleazy because he thought I was you, after seeing you practice your cheers. I bet you were doing everything short of landing your cartwheels on his chest to make sure he noticed you."

"Cartwheels on chest," Jessica said with a laugh, pretending she was writing it down on her hand. "Sounds effective. I'll add that to my list of ways to get guys' attention."

Elizabeth didn't want to like Brad Cotter, but Jessica was right. She hated to judge a person based on nothing more than a first impression. "If he thought that you'd already come on to him—and that I was you—then maybe he had a halfway decent reason for acting like a conceited jerk with me," Elizabeth conceded.

"Speaking of conceited jerks, Heather the Horrible butted into my conversation with Brad before I could get any useful information," complained her sister. "So I hardly know anything about him. *You* talked to him. Tell me more! What kind of car does he drive?"

Elizabeth shrugged, turning the Jeep onto Calico Drive. "I don't know! I think he's got a rental car this week. We talked about the *Scoop* story and about how I want to keep our relationship strictly professional. That's all."

"I thought you journalists were supposed to have a nose for news! At least tell me where he's staying while he's in town."

"I'm a journalist, not a bloodhound," Elizabeth replied. "How should I know where he's staying? Probably in the fanciest suite at the fanciest hotel he can find. On Daddy's credit card."

Jessica stared at her. "Are you saying Daddy Cotter has money?" she asked, a little breathless. "Cowabunga! Brad is looking better and better every minute!"

"Brad's father is one of the owners of CCB

Media," Elizabeth explained. "That's the media giant that runs *Scoop,* among other things."

Jessica's smile broadened. "Now I am *definitely* in love!"

"You just said you hardly know anything about Brad," Elizabeth reminded her.

"You're always saying how important it is to learn new things!"

Elizabeth shook her head. "I think we should change the subject before I get sick."

"OK, let's talk about dinner," Jessica said. "I'm starved. Are we still on for Guido's?"

"I can already taste the pizza," Elizabeth told her. "Oh, I forgot to tell you I invited Todd to come with us."

"That should be a thrill a minute."

"You'll survive," Elizabeth said. "Besides, Todd offered to drive. You know you like riding in his BMW."

"Not when I feel like I'm chaperoning you on a date!" Jessica moaned. "There are limits, Liz—even when a Beemer's involved. Anyway, I need to go to Lila's house first. I can't go out to dinner until I tell her I met Brad!"

"Todd can pick me up here in a half hour, like we planned," Elizabeth suggested, pulling the Jeep into the Wakefield family's driveway. "Meanwhile you take the Jeep to Lila's. You can meet us at Guido's when you're finished gabbing about the guy du jour."

"Come on, Liz," Jessica urged as soon as she slid into the booth beside Todd at Guido's on Wednesday night. "Tell me everything you know about Brad Cotter."

Elizabeth shook her head. "I already told you—I don't know anything."

"You must know something!" Jessica insisted. "For instance, how old is he?"

"Well, he said he's putting off college while he works at *Scoop*. So I'd guess he's around twenty, give or take a couple years."

"I could have guessed that just from looking at him." Jessica sighed. "What good is it, having a sister with access to a good-looking guy, if the sister is too clueless to take advantage of the situation?"

"It may surprise you to learn that I have business with Brad Cotter that has nothing to do with helping you throw yourself at him."

"That is lame, Liz!" Todd chastised her in a teasing voice. "You've forgotten that Jessica is the center of the universe and the rest of us just revolve around her."

"Grow a personality, Wilkins," Jessica said, scowling at him. "And for your information, Elizabeth, I don't want you to help me throw myself at Brad. I want you to help me to help him throw *himself* at me!"

"That last sentence is making me dizzy," Todd complained.

"Face it, Liz," Jessica said. "Your priorities are completely postal when it comes to Brad. You don't even seem to notice that he's a total hunk! Maybe you should have your eyes checked."

"Her eyes are just fine!" Todd put in, sounding alarmed.

"Will it make you feel better if I admit it?" Elizabeth asked her sister. "I will: Brad Cotter is astonishingly handsome. Are you happy now?"

Todd's eyebrows shot up. "*I'm* not happy!" he said. "Do you mean that, Liz?"

"Well, *sort of* astonishingly handsome," Elizabeth modified. "In a sleazy kind of way."

"And you're going to be working with this guy?" Todd asked, his face twisted into a frown. Jessica grinned.

"I don't care about his looks, Todd!" Elizabeth exclaimed. She smiled warmly. "He's not nearly as astonishingly handsome as you are. Besides, Brad's looks are totally offset by his obnoxious personality."

Yeah, thought Jessica. *The way Todd's good looks are totally offset by his* bland *personality.* "Lighten up, Liz," she said. "You're a disgrace to teenage girls everywhere."

Elizabeth shook her head in mock sadness. "I'm so embarrassed," she replied. "Does this mean I lose my membership in Boy Crazy Anonymous?"

Jessica stared at her thoughtfully. "That depends on you," she said. "Find out more about Brad, and I won't tear up your membership card."

"Now *there's* some incentive," Elizabeth countered.

"Aw, come on, Lizzie," Jessica pleaded. "You're my only sister—my only identical twin sister, who would do anything for me. All you have to do is keep your ears open when you're around Brad, maybe ask him a question every now and then, and report back to me about what you learn."

Suddenly Elizabeth's face grew thoughtful. "I'll do it!" she announced.

"You will?" asked Jessica and Todd together.

"On one condition," Elizabeth said, staring at her twin.

"This isn't about bringing up my grade in algebra, is it?"

"No," Elizabeth replied.

"Making dinner when it's my turn instead of letting you do it for me?"

"Well, that would be nice. But no."

"Getting your blue blouse dry-cleaned to remove the chocolate syrup stains I dripped?"

"What chocolate syrup stains?" Elizabeth demanded. "When did you wear my blue blouse?"

"Oops," said Jessica. "I could've sworn I'd mentioned that before."

Elizabeth shook her head hopelessly. "You *will* have that blouse cleaned," she told her twin in a menacing tone. "But that's not my condition."

"What is?" Jessica asked, anxious to get Elizabeth's mind off that blouse.

"I promise to find out what I can about Brad," Elizabeth pledged. "But in exchange I want you to ask Ms. Swanson to be faculty adviser to the cheerleading squad."

"*Huh?*"

"You heard me!" Elizabeth said.

"I know *what* you said, I just don't know *why* you said it," Jessica explained. "Who is this Ms. Swanson?"

"She's the new library lady who started at Sweet Valley High this year," Todd answered.

"Oh, *her,*" Jessica said. "I've seen her around, always trying to look like she's invisible." Then she turned on Todd. "Since when are you Mr. Library Science?" Jessica asked.

Todd shrugged. "Ms. Swanson helped me find references for my history paper. She was really quiet, like she was afraid of people. But she was totally nice, and she knows a lot about research."

"Knows a lot about research," Jessica mused slowly. "Now there's a good qualification for a cheerleading adviser. You know how it is. You're in the middle of a back handspring, and you suddenly need to know who Aristotle was. At times like that, it's comforting to have a librarian on the squad."

"You don't have anyone else in mind for adviser, do you?" Elizabeth challenged.

Jessica shook her head. "Not yet," she admitted. "The teachers are all just too uncool."

"So what have you got to lose?" Elizabeth asked. "You have to find a faculty adviser. That's the rule. And you won't find anyone with as much school spirit as Ms. Swanson."

"She never misses a basketball game for either the girls' or boys' team," Todd pointed out.

"But she's a wimpy little mouse!" Jessica protested. "She can barely speak above a whisper!"

"That shouldn't matter," Elizabeth said. "It's not like the faculty adviser has to be able to scream out the Funky Monkey cheer on the football field during a game."

"I know that," Jessica shot back. "But we're a *championship* squad. We have a reputation to uphold! She had to be a total loser when she was in high school."

"Jessica, the truth is she's shy and lonely," Elizabeth said. "But she loves this school, and she wants to fit in. Being asked to work with the cheerleaders will help her feel that she belongs."

"She *belongs* in a mental institution if she thinks someone who's afraid of her own shadow can lead a squad of independent-minded cheerleaders. She'd be too shy to tell us what to do or—"

Jessica stopped, realizing what she was saying. Suddenly she began to laugh. She threw her arms around her sister. "That's it!" she screamed. "Liz, you're a genius! Ms. Swanson is perfect! She's stupendous! What an awesome find!"

If anyone is going to be a pushover, Jessica thought, *it'll be the timid assistant librarian.* The other girls would be totally relieved.

Chapter 5

"I can't believe I'm spending my lunch period in the school library!" Lila complained as she slammed her locker door on Thursday and joined three of the other cheerleaders in the hallway. "I should be out in the courtyard, working on my tan."

"This won't take the whole lunch period," Maria assured her. "At least I hope it won't."

"If Elizabeth is right about the assistant librarian, it will hardly take any convincing at all," Jessica said. "Liz thinks Ms. Swanson will be thrilled to be our adviser!"

Heather rolled her eyes. "And what makes you think Elizabeth is right? For that matter, why should Elizabeth care who sponsors us? She dropped off the squad."

"Elizabeth is a do-gooder," Jessica explained. "She thinks this will make Ms. Swanson feel needed or something."

"She *is* needed," Maria said. "We have to find a cheerleading adviser, whether we want to or not."

"If Elizabeth cares so much, why isn't she here helping us?" Heather asked.

"I don't know," Jessica replied. "She's probably out somewhere boring with her boring boyfriend, Todd. Or her boring friends Enid and Maria."

Maria looked up.

"I mean the *other* Maria," Jessica said quickly. "Maria Slater, not Santelli."

"Whatever," Heather said. "Are we sure this library geek Nancy Swanson isn't going to be a pain in the neck?" she asked, stopping them all outside the library door. "What if she's a control freak?"

Maria shook her head. "No way! I know Ms. Swanson. She's just like Elizabeth said, sweet and shy. I don't see her turning into Sergeant Cheerleader."

"We're trusting Elizabeth's judgment a lot on this one," Heather cautioned. "Of course, *Jessica* trusts her. But I'm the other cocaptain. Shouldn't I have equal say?"

Lila couldn't take another minute of Heather's whining. "Look, Heather. For once in your life would you just shut up? This is not about getting your own way. This is about damage control."

"It's not like you've thought of anyone else to ask instead of Ms. Swanson," Jessica pointed out to Heather. "We are running out of options."

Heather sighed loudly.

"Heather, we're just going in to talk," Maria

said in a reasonable voice. "We'll give it a few minutes so you can see what you think. If you're still skeptical after you meet her, just give me the signal, and we won't ask her just yet."

"We only have until tomorrow to find someone," Lila reminded her.

"True," Maria said. "But Heather *is* a cocaptain. We can't ignore her opinion. If we four don't all agree on Ms. Swanson after a few minutes of talking to her, then we'll get the whole squad together this afternoon and discuss it again."

Jessica nodded. "OK, we can always ask Ms. Swanson tomorrow if we still can't think of anyone better."

"I'm sure we won't need to," Maria said, pushing open the library door. "I think Heather is going to love her!"

A few minutes later the four girls were standing around the reference desk, talking to the assistant librarian.

"What a nice surprise!" Ms. Swanson said, pushing her long brown hair behind one ear. "I've been meaning to tell you what a great job you did, cheering at the field hockey game last weekend! That maneuver with the consecutive stag leaps was perfectly timed."

Heather beamed. "Thank you," she said. "I choreographed that one."

Lila saw Jessica roll her eyes.

"And Jessica, I've never seen such a complicated back-flip combination executed as beautifully as

71

that move you did the last time we scored!"

This time Heather rolled her eyes.

"The whole squad has been amazing this year," Ms. Swanson continued, blushing as she raised a hand to cover her mouth. "We were all so proud of you, making it all the way to the national cheerleading competition."

"Thanks," Maria said. "We were all pretty excited too. Just being at the competition was an incredible experience—"

"True," Heather broke in. "It's been more than twenty years since Sweet Valley had a cheerleading squad at nationals. It wasn't until I transferred here—"

"Well, you girls are much better than the 1976 squad," Ms. Swanson interrupted pleasantly.

"You saw the Girls of Seventy-six in action?" Jessica asked. "I didn't know you grew up in Sweet Valley."

"Oh, yes, I moved away for a while, but I'm from here originally," Ms. Swanson replied. "But I know that's not what you came here to talk to me about."

Lila saw Heather nod eagerly at Maria. Obviously the assistant librarian's flattery had convinced the reluctant cocaptain.

"Actually we have a big favor to ask you," Maria said to Ms. Swanson, pulling out her student council clipboard. "Of course you've heard about the new rule requiring student organizations to have faculty advisers."

"We want you to be the cheerleading adviser!" Jessica blurted.

72

Ms. Swanson's blue eyes opened wide. "You want *me?* But I thought you didn't . . . I mean—"

"We originally thought of you because you're so, uh, *nice,*" Jessica explained. "Everyone likes you."

"And you've got more school spirit than anyone else on the faculty," Lila added. This meeting was beginning to be a total bore, but she'd promised Jessica she would help.

"Now that we've talked to you, we can see we've made the right choice," Heather said. "You obviously know something about cheerleading. I doubt any other staff member at this school could tell a stag leap from a herky."

Maria scanned the guidelines on her clipboard. "As adviser, you would have to be present at every game. And you're required to meet with us at least once a month as well."

"But there's no rule that says you have to come to every practice," Heather added quickly.

Jessica nodded vigorously. "We wouldn't want this to be too big a time commitment for you."

"Besides that, you'd be a resource for us and a liaison with the faculty and administration," Maria concluded.

"Will you do it?" Jessica asked. "Please?"

The assistant librarian's hand flew to her mouth again. Her face was almost as red as the cheerleading uniform Jessica was wearing. "I don't know what to say," she mumbled. "I never thought—"

"Say yes," Heather urged. "I swear it won't be

too much extra work for you. We pretty much run ourselves."

"All right," Ms. Swanson agreed. "I would be honored." She was blinking as if she was afraid she might cry. But Lila was sure she saw a smile under the woman's hand.

"I might even have some ideas for things you might do with your uniforms and routines," Ms. Swanson continued. She stopped, looking at Heather and Jessica. "Just as suggestions, I mean. Of course, I'd never presume to tell you how to run your squad—"

Jessica visibly relaxed. "I think we're going to get along just fine," she said.

A few minutes later Ms. Swanson had signed Maria's forms and the girls were walking down the hallway toward the cafeteria.

"Wow!" Maria said. "Did you see how happy she was? I swear I could see tears in her eyes when we asked."

"That woman needs to get a life," Lila observed.

"Why *shouldn't* she be happy?" Heather asked. "She's now the adviser to the number-two cheerleading squad in the nation. I don't blame her for being psyched!"

"What's with the way she puts her hand over her face all the time?" Maria asked.

"Elizabeth says some shy people do that because they're embarrassed about showing emotions," Jessica replied.

Lila shook her head. "I bet she just has really awful teeth!" She wrinkled her nose. "How vile."

"I'm sure you can put up with it for a few weeks," Maria said.

"It's not like you're a permanent member of the squad," Heather reminded her.

"Don't worry, Heather," Lila said. "If I can put up with you, I can certainly put up with a mousy librarian with gross teeth."

"I don't care what her teeth look like!" Jessica declared. "Ms. Swanson is the find of the century. There's no way she'll ever try to tell us what to do. This is going to be great!"

"You were right about Ms. Swanson," Jessica told her sister at the dinner table that night. "She's going to be the perfect cheerleading adviser."

Elizabeth grinned. She was glad everything was working out the way she'd wanted it to. "How did she react when you asked her?"

"She was stoked," Jessica said, spooning salsa into her taco. "Like she could hardly believe we'd chosen her. It was almost pathetic."

"Now, Jessica, is that a nice thing to say?" asked Mrs. Wakefield, passing Elizabeth the guacamole.

"Ms. Swanson doesn't have much self-confidence," Elizabeth explained. "But she cares a lot about the school. Asking her to help with the cheerleading squad is one of the nicest things anyone could do for her."

"Jessica, I can't believe you asked her just out of the goodness of your heart," said the twins' older brother. Steven, a freshman at nearby Sweet Valley University, was home for a long weekend. "Out with it, Jess. You must have had an ulterior motive."

Jessica took a drink of her diet soda. "Of course I had an ulterior motive," she said. "Do I look stupid?"

Steven opened his mouth to reply, but Jessica cut him off. "The truth is, I made a deal with Elizabeth. I do the Samaritan thing with Ms. Scared-of-her-own-shadow, and Liz helps me find out more about a certain hunky guy."

Steven groaned. "I should have guessed there was a boy involved."

"As it turned out, asking Ms. Swanson was a terrific idea," Jessica said. "We couldn't have found a better adviser."

"Does that mean you're not holding me to my end of our deal?" Elizabeth asked.

"Bite your tongue!" Jessica said with a grin. "But I admit Ms. Swanson isn't nearly as geeky as I thought she was. She says she can see we know what we're doing, so she isn't going to ram any new rules down our throats."

"Are those the preferred qualifications in a cheerleading adviser?" Mr. Wakefield asked. "Nongeekiness, flattery of the cheerleaders, and a reluctance to make rules?"

"Absolutely!" Jessica replied with a smile. "But Ms. Swanson surprised us all with another qualification. She actually *knows* something about cheerleading."

"It must be from all those games she goes to," Elizabeth said, helping herself to some refried beans.

"Did you know she was here in 1976, when those other Sweet Valley High cheerleaders were state champs?" Jessica asked.

Elizabeth's spoonful of refried beans stopped halfway to her plate. "I didn't know she grew up in Sweet Valley. She never mentioned it."

"It's not like faculty members are in the habit of telling students about their childhoods," Steven pointed out.

"It only kind of slipped out today that she'd seen the Girls of Seventy-six cheer," Jessica said. "By the way, she says our squad is tons better!"

"Does that mean she knew those girls you're looking up for the magazine article, Liz?" Mrs. Wakefield asked.

Jessica shrugged. "She didn't exactly say that she *knew* them. Knowing Ms. Swanson, I can't believe she was the type to hang out with cool people like cheerleaders."

"We can't all be blessed," Steven said wryly.

"I'm surprised she didn't mention it yesterday. I told her what I was researching." Elizabeth tried hard to recall her conversation with the assistant librarian. "I guess we got steered onto other topics before she had the chance."

"So how is the research going?" Jessica asked.

Elizabeth blinked. "What's this? *You're* asking a question about *me?* Jessica Wakefield cares about someone besides herself?"

Jessica shrugged. "Only if the research is on something interesting."

"Well, I didn't have time to get to the library today to scour those old yearbooks for more clues, but I plan to go tomorrow."

"What have you found so far?" her father asked.

"Apparently at least three of the girls are still in Sweet Valley, and—"

"This is fascinating, Elizabeth, but it's not exactly the research I was talking about," Jessica interrupted. "Nobody cares about cheerleaders from prehistoric times. I meant your research on Brad!"

Mr. Wakefield leaned forward in his chair. "Brad who?"

"Would that be the latest Hunk of the Week?" Steven asked.

"Sorry, Jess, but I still don't know much about him," Elizabeth admitted.

"You must know something," Jessica said. "Like, what's he been doing in his free time while he's here?"

Elizabeth shook her head. "I don't know."

"Who does he like better, me or Heather?"

Jessica asked, her blue-green eyes worried. "I know it's me. Isn't it? I can tell by the way he practically ignored Heather in the hallway yesterday. Well, maybe he didn't ignore her, exactly. He was polite. But he almost came right out and said he'd rather let *me* show him around town. So why hasn't he called? You don't think Heather got to him, do you? I wouldn't put it past that conniving little twerp—"

Elizabeth glanced at Steven, and they both burst into laughter. "Jessica, you are too much," Elizabeth said.

"Who is this Brad person?" their father asked again.

"He's gorgeous!" Jessica replied. "What's his schedule like while he's here, Liz? And have you found out where he's staying yet? Don't you have a number where you can get hold of him in case you learn anything important in your research?"

"No, I don't," Elizabeth told her twin. "He'll contact me at school tomorrow. Besides, Jessica, my research is on ex-cheerleaders, not immature party boys."

"But you promised!" Jessica protested.

"Yes, I did, and I'll tell you when I have some information. But at the moment I don't know anything more about Brad than I knew yesterday."

"Brad who?" asked Mr. Wakefield.

Chapter 6

The last class of the day had ended, but the school library was still open Friday afternoon as Elizabeth plunked three yearbooks onto a table in the corner. Enid Rollins pushed a lock of coppery brown hair behind one ear and pulled the top book from the stack. She and Maria Slater were there to help their friend with her research for *Scoop*.

Elizabeth opened the yearbook to the official cheerleading squad photograph. "Here they are, the Girls of Seventy-six," Elizabeth said. Eight girls posed with their red-and-white pom-poms. A megaphone was appliquéd on the front of each uniform beneath a big SVH, and all the girls wore very short split skirts.

"The 1976 California State Championship Cheerleading Squad," Enid read aloud.

Maria's big brown eyes danced with glee in her beautiful, coffee-colored face. The African

American girl looked around the room melodramatically, as if to make sure they were alone. Sure enough, Ms. Swanson had stepped into the librarian's office. Nobody else was around. Maria pretended she was running a hand through a mane of wild, ash blond curls instead of her own short, sleek black ones. Enid recognized the gesture: pure Heather Mallone.

"'Come on, everybody, do the Funky Monkey!'" Maria recited in a quieter imitation of Heather's cheering voice, waving her arms.

"'SVH is rockin', we're groovin' and we're hunky!'" Elizabeth continued for her, impersonating Jessica.

Enid was giggling so hard, she nearly fell off her chair. "Liz, we all saw you playing cheerleader for a few weeks, and you were great at it," she said when she had her laughter under control. "But it is so hard to imagine you jumping around on a football field, yelling things like that."

"It's hard for me to believe it too," Elizabeth replied. "I'm just glad my cheerleading days are over."

"Surely you miss the intellectual challenge of spelling out letters with your arms," Maria said sarcastically.

"True," Elizabeth joked. "Sometimes when I'm alone in my room, I still get the urge to do '*R-O-W-D-I-E!* That's the way we spell *rowdy!*'"

"That's the way *Jessica* spells it, maybe," Enid said.

"Do you think the Girls of Seventy-six had to chant such idiotic things?" Maria asked.

"Probably," Elizabeth said. "Look at this cheer they've reprinted in the yearbook. You two join in on the audience-participation part!" She pointed to the words and began impersonating Jessica's voice again. "'Are you rootin' for the boys?'"

"Yeah, man!" replied Maria and Enid.

"'Are you making any noise?'" Elizabeth asked.

"'Sure am!'"

"'Are we gonna win tonight?'"

"'You're doggone right!'" Maria and Enid exclaimed, their voices dissolving into laughter.

"'If we fight, if we fight! If we fight, fight, fight!'" Elizabeth concluded.

All three girls were laughing so hard that Ms. Swanson poked her head out the door of the office for a moment. Seeing only Elizabeth, Maria, and Enid, she stepped back inside, but Enid noticed she kept the door cracked. *Probably thinks she needs to keep an eye on us,* Enid thought.

"Oops!" Maria said, still giggling.

"I love that 'yeah, man' part!" Enid said. "Can you believe people really talked that way?"

"I guess we've answered my question about whether the 1976 cheerleaders had to recite ditzy lines," Maria said. "I guess a cheerleader has always been a cheerleader—no matter what decade!"

"Despite the bonehead words to the cheers, one thing I realized from my cheerleading days is that cheering is a lot harder than it looks,"

82

Elizabeth admitted a few minutes later. She'd always thought of cheerleaders more as decorations than athletes, but her experience on the squad had taught her otherwise. She pointed to the yearbook photograph. "It took a lot of skill and practice for these girls to win the state championship in 1976, and it still does for Jessica and her friends."

"So which of these cheerleaders have been located so far?" Maria asked, pointing to the squad photo.

Elizabeth recognized one of the girls without even reading the caption. "The tall blonde on the right is Diane Norton, the *Scoop* reporter I'm helping with this story. She's hardly changed a bit—except that her hair is shorter and permed now."

Enid read the caption. "It says the girl in the middle, with the big hair, is the head cheerleader," she said. "Loretta Bari. She was a senior that year. Is she still in Sweet Valley?"

"I don't know," Elizabeth replied. "I tried to look her up in the phone book last night and couldn't find her."

"She might have gotten married and changed her name," Enid suggested.

"Which ones have you found?" Maria asked.

Elizabeth scrutinized the picture. "These three—Susan Mendel, Gail Jackson, and Kelly Shaw—are living in Sweet Valley. And we've got Diane, of course."

"So Loretta Bari is still a mystery," Enid said.

"And so are the other three—Claire Lyons, Rosalia Martinez, and May Eng," Maria added.

Elizabeth ran her hand over the picture. "Yes, but I'm sure we'll track them down."

"Mr. Cooper's secretary probably has phone numbers for all the class-reunion committees," Enid said thoughtfully. "Whoever plans the reunions for their classes might know how to contact them."

Elizabeth grinned. "Enid, you're a genius!"

"Hey, girlfriends," said Maria, turning to another section of the yearbook. "Get a load of this!" She jabbed her finger at a photograph of several couples. Every girl had long black hair—most of them obviously wearing wigs. And every boy wore a fake mustache.

"A Sonny and Cher look-alike contest!" Enid sang out. "That's hysterical!"

"The girl who played Cher in the winning team is one of my missing cheerleaders," Elizabeth noticed. "Her name is Claire Lyons—though in her other photos she's a strawberry blonde."

"And look at the guy who won as Sonny Bono," Maria said, pointing to the middle couple. "It says his name is Thomas Egbert! That's not Winston's dad, is it?"

"No, Mr. Egbert is tall and skinny, like Winston," Elizabeth replied with a chuckle. "Besides, he's too old to have been in high school in 1976. I think Winston mentioned an Uncle Tom once, though I'm sure he doesn't live around here anymore."

"He looks kind of like Winston," Enid observed. "If you can imagine a short Winston with a cheap-looking fake mustache."

"Obviously Tom knew Claire Lyons when they were in high school," Elizabeth said. "I'll ask Winston to see if his uncle has kept in touch with her. Maybe he knows how to find her today."

Enid opened the 1975 yearbook to a random page. "Here are some prom photos," she said. "Powder blue tuxedos! What a scream!"

"Far out!" Maria said, laughing.

"Groovy!" Elizabeth added.

"Those funny eyeglasses with the thick black rims are total tacko," Maria said. "But almost every kid with glasses is wearing that style." She thumbed through the 1976 edition. "Speaking of style, how about those basketball uniforms?" She wiggled her eyebrows at Elizabeth.

"Their shorts are *so short!*" Elizabeth exclaimed.

"And tight," Maria added in a mischievous tone.

"They look weird compared to the long, baggy shorts the guys wear now," Elizabeth said, nodding. "But I can see some definite advantages!"

Maria laughed. "You're just imagining Todd Wilkins with his long, muscular legs showing."

"I wouldn't mind seeing that," Elizabeth said. "Strictly in the interest of research, of course."

"Of course," Enid agreed. "You'd understand the 1976 cheerleaders much better if you could see boys who looked like the athletes they cheered for back then."

"Just don't let Todd grow his hair out like these boys!" Maria said. "Fluffy is fine if you're a cat. But it's not a good look for a boyfriend."

"Most Likely to Date John Travolta," Enid read aloud from the 1976 yearbook.

"He was a babe back then," Maria said with a smile.

"He's still pretty hot," Enid replied. "Anyway, your ex-cheerleader friend Diane Norton won that honor, Liz."

Elizabeth laughed. "We'll have to find a way to get that into the *Scoop* story!"

"I loved Travolta in *Grease*," Maria said with a sigh. "The Travolta look *ruled* the late seventies."

"I forgot we had an entertainment-industry expert in our midst," Enid said. "A real live TV star!"

Maria rolled her eyes. "Being the Softee Toilet Paper kid doesn't qualify me for TV star status."

"And you did movies and television," Enid reminded her. "Don't be modest."

"Not to mention being the Macaroni Princess for Princess brand macaroni," Elizabeth added. "You certainly got more than your allotted fifteen minutes of fame."

"But I've been away from Hollywood since I was twelve."

"Even so, here's another bit of seventies Hollywood trivia you probably know more about than I do," Enid said, pointing to another page in the yearbook. "It's a poll taken of all the girls at SVH. Who Do You Dig More: Starsky or Hutch?"

"Definitely Starsky," Maria said.

"No way!" argued Elizabeth. "Hutch was much better looking!"

"They were TV cops," Maria explained, noting Enid's bewildered expression. "One was tall, blond, and cute. The other was short, dark haired, and even cuter."

"So *you're* a popular-culture expert too," Enid said to Elizabeth. "I feel so ignorant compared to you two."

"I saw a rerun once," Elizabeth told her friend with a shrug. She pointed to another yearbook photograph. "Look, SVH hosted the regional basketball tournament that year, and it had a bicentennial theme: Philadelphia Freedom."

"That's an old Elton John song," Enid announced. Elizabeth looked at her in surprise. "I'm better at music than television," Enid explained.

"It wasn't an *old* song in 1976," Maria reminded them. "Look at the school gym decorated in red, white, and blue. They even had fireworks outside after we won the final game of the tournament."

"And here's the cheerleading squad at that game, waving American flags instead of pompoms," Enid said. She began to turn the page, but Elizabeth stopped her hand.

"Wait a minute," Elizabeth said slowly. "That squad isn't the same as the one in the shot from the first football game of the year. I'm sure this Asian girl from the basketball game wasn't in the football shot."

Maria flipped back through the yearbook. "She is in the official team photo," she said. "Her name's May Eng. Maybe she was sick the day of the first football game. Or maybe she joined the squad after football season started."

"It's not like we haven't had any turnover among the cheerleaders this year," Enid reminded them.

Elizabeth nodded. "I'll say! It's like the squad has a revolving door. I'm just glad I revolved out of it."

She noticed Nancy Swanson pushing a cart of books across the library toward them. "You know, Jessica said Ms. Swanson was a student here when those girls cheered. Let's go talk to her. Maybe she'll remember more about them."

"I'd love to stick around and find out," Enid said, checking her watch. "But I need to get home. I promised my mom I'd be home early enough to start dinner for her. She's having some people over tonight."

Maria sighed. "And I have a date with Ted Jensen tonight. I have to go figure out what to wear."

After her friends had left, Elizabeth approached the assistant librarian, who was shelving books nearby. She held up the yearbook. "I didn't realize you knew the Girls of Seventy-six," she said.

Ms. Swanson froze as if she'd been startled. She stood facing Elizabeth, with a book in each of her outstretched hands. Her lips twitched into a tense frown. "I didn't!" she protested quickly. "Well, I guess I did, sort of, but not very well. I didn't mention it the other day because I knew I couldn't help with your story. I don't know where those girls are. We don't keep in touch."

As Ms. Swanson spoke, her face twisted into an expression Elizabeth couldn't read.

"Are you OK?" Elizabeth asked. "You look so . . . tense."

The woman turned to the bookshelf. "It's nothing," she said in a quiet, controlled voice. "I have a toothache, that's all."

"Maybe you should see a dentist," Elizabeth suggested, sorry that the sweet, timid woman was in pain.

"I'm sorry, Elizabeth," the assistant librarian continued in the same strange voice. "I'd like to talk, but I can't right now. I have so many books to put away. . . ."

"No problem," Elizabeth replied, feeling distinctly uncomfortable in Ms. Swanson's presence. "I've got to be going anyway."

What was that all about? Elizabeth wondered as she gathered her things and left the library. *Ms. Swanson looked like she'd seen a ghost!*

Chapter 7

Jessica watched Tim Nelson's broad back as he disappeared into the crowd of teenagers at the Beach Disco on Saturday night. She turned to join Lila and Amy at their table.

"OK, the guys are getting us sodas," she said, wiping her perspiring forehead with a napkin. "Now we can gossip."

"Tim looks great tonight, Jess!" Amy said, raising her voice to be heard above the taped music that was playing while the band took a break. "I didn't know he could dance."

"Who would have thought?" Lila asked. "I mean, the guy is a linebacker. I wasn't sure he'd advanced to the concept of right and left, except for on the football field."

"Tim's OK," Jessica said. "I mean, at least the architecture is solid, even if the attic is empty."

Lila laughed. "Jess, you're too much!"

"People tell me that a lot," Jessica replied.

"I was noticing his architecture too," Amy said. "What a build! But you're not serious about him, are you?" Jessica could practically see the gossip antennae sprouting from her straight blond hair.

"No way!" Jessica exclaimed. "He's just fun for an occasional date."

"He is awesomely cute!" Amy said. "Well, not as cute as Barry," she added, defending her longtime boyfriend, Barry Rork.

"And *nobody* is as cute as Bo," Lila murmured, a dreamy smile replacing her usually cool demeanor.

"Nobody is as *rich* as Bo," Jessica corrected. "Except you."

"Rich, cute, it's the same thing," Lila said. Because he lived on the East Coast, Bo didn't get to visit as often as Lila would have liked. But his father had business in Los Angeles that weekend and had brought Bo along to see Lila.

"Speaking of cute guys, Jessica, have you seen that photographer, Brad, since Wednesday?" Amy asked.

Jessica slumped back in her chair. "No!" she wailed. "My lucky sister was supposed to go interview some ex-cheerleader with him today. But I haven't seen him at all in the last three days!"

"I thought he said he wanted you to show him around town," Amy said.

"He did," Jessica replied, folding her arms in

front of her. "I just hope he's busy working on that cheerleader story."

"As opposed to being busy having a certain cheerleader working on him?" Lila guessed.

Amy shook her head. "What are you talking about?"

"It's not a *what*, it's a *who*," Lila answered. "Heather."

"You were right the first time," Jessica said glumly. "Heather is definitely not a *who*. She's not even human. She's an insect. A big, blond praying mantis in a cheerleading uniform."

"Do you think Brad is spending his time with her?" Amy asked.

Jessica bit her lip. "I don't know," she admitted. "Heather was all secretive about some date she was supposedly going on after we cheered at the soccer match last night. I assumed she was making up the whole thing. Maybe I was wrong. Maybe she went out with Brad."

Lila was gazing intently across the room. "I don't know about last night, but she's got a date tonight," she said. "And it's *not* with Brad Cotter."

"Heather's here?" Jessica exclaimed, whirling in her seat. "Where? Who's she with?" Her hand flew to her mouth. "This is *not* happening!"

"Jeffrey French?" Lila asked incredulously. "I could have sworn he had better taste than that. Even if he *did* go steady with Elizabeth when Todd moved away."

"Watch it!" Jessica warned, narrowing her eyes. "Elizabeth happens to be one of the prettiest girls at school. One of the *two* prettiest."

"Your modesty is overwhelming, Ms. Identical Twin," Lila said.

Jessica smiled sweetly. "You taught me everything I know."

"Ha, ha," said Lila. "But I wasn't talking about Elizabeth's looks. I was talking about her personality."

"You have a point," Jessica conceded. "My sister *could* stand to loosen up a little. But Elizabeth is a million times more fun than Heather the Horrible. How could Jeffrey do this to her?"

"She's the one who dumped Jeffrey when Todd moved back to town," Amy reminded her. "Why shouldn't he go out with Heather?"

Because I was in love with him too! Jessica wanted to say. But nobody knew that she'd been in love with her sister's boyfriend for a time. Of course, she'd gotten over Jeffrey. She had no claim on him at all. But it still steamed her to see Heather hanging on the arm of the handsome blond soccer player.

"Because she's a bossy, manipulative brat," Lila answered Amy. "Not at all Jeffrey's type."

"You're right about that," Jessica said.

"Will Elizabeth freak out?" Amy asked, her gray eyes lighting up the way they always did when she sensed a juicy piece of gossip.

"I guess not," Jessica replied. "She'll probably wish it was anyone but Heather, but I don't think she'll really be upset. Liz is *so* over him. She barely mentions him at all anymore."

"It doesn't look serious between Jeffrey and Heather, if you ask me," Lila observed. "She's flirting like crazy—I can see it from here. And Jeffrey looks like he's having a good time, but it's not like he's hanging on her every word."

"True," Amy said with a giggle. "He's talking to Winston Egbert now. No guy would turn away from a girl he really liked in order to have a gab fest with a drip like Winston."

On the one hand, Jessica would have preferred to see her cocaptain on a date with the president of the school chess team or a member of the electronics club. On the other hand, it was a relief to know for sure that Heather was spending the evening with someone other than Brad. *Anyone* but Brad.

But that still doesn't mean he likes me, she admitted to herself. And she'd been so sure that he did.

Elizabeth sat at a table in the school library on Monday, poring over a leather-bound volume of *Oracle* issues from the seventies. The collection was far from complete, but it did contain all the special graduation issues from the seventies, which were proving to be a gold mine of cheerleader information.

Suddenly somebody grabbed Elizabeth from behind. A pair of hands covered her eyes.

"Hey!" she yelled, twisting in her chair. Then

she laughed with relief. "Todd, it's you! You nearly gave me a heart attack!"

"It's lunch period, not study hall," Todd said. "Come back to the cafeteria with me. I brought an extra sandwich."

"No, thanks, Todd," Elizabeth said. "I've got a lot of work to do here."

"It's tuna fish!"

"I grabbed a yogurt before I came down here."

"Yogurt? That's health food—not fit for human consumption. How about cookies? I know chocolate chip is your favorite. I'll make you a deal. Come with me, and you can have half my cookies. They're homemade."

"Thanks, but no," Elizabeth said with a smile. "I've found these old issues of the *Oracle*, and they're a tremendous source of leads on the Girls of Seventy-six."

"No excuses," he said, pulling out the chair next to her and straddling it. "I'm officially kidnapping you and bringing you back to the cafeteria. Or the school courtyard, if you'd prefer."

Elizabeth rolled her eyes. "Kidnapping?"

Todd shrugged. "I figure it's the only way I'll ever get to spend any time with you. I didn't see you all weekend, you were so busy with this *Scoop* thing."

"This '*Scoop* thing' is an article in a national magazine," Elizabeth reminded him. "I know it's taking a lot of time, but it's important."

"Even Winston said you stopped by his house

on Saturday," Todd grumbled. "But you didn't have time for me."

"Get over it, Todd. You're not honestly worried about *Winston* as competition, are you?"

Todd shook his head. "Of course not. But it was a long, cold, lonely weekend." He put his hand to his forehead in a melodramatic gesture.

"Poor baby," Elizabeth said. She pecked him on the cheek. "I'm sorry I've been so busy, but I'll be finished by the end of the week. And Winston was really helpful. He gave me his uncle Tom's phone number, and I called Tom about one of the cheerleaders he was friends with back in 1976."

She pulled the 1976 yearbook across the table and opened it to the cheerleading squad photograph. "This is the girl," she said, pointing. "Her name is Claire Lyons. She was a senior that year, like Winston's uncle. Now she runs a casino in Reno with her husband."

"Fascinating."

"And I found out from the 1978 graduation issue of the *Oracle* that May Eng was planning to study drama at Sweet Valley University."

"Why 1978?" Todd asked. "I thought these were the Girls of Seventy-six."

"Well, 1976 was the year they won the state cheerleading championship," she explained. "But they weren't all seniors that year. May was the only sophomore. She didn't graduate until 1978."

"I get it," Todd said. "Doesn't this stuff bore

you stiff? I mean, you didn't know these girls. How exciting can it be, finding out that they're in Reno or wherever?"

"Some of them are doing some really interesting things," Elizabeth replied. "May Eng, for instance. A few minutes ago I called the drama department at SVU, and the secretary looked up her records for me."

"I didn't think they were allowed to give out student information like that over the phone," Todd said.

"She wasn't allowed to tell me much," Elizabeth admitted. "She did say that May transferred to NYU on a drama scholarship in her junior year. So I logged onto the Internet and found her through an actors' association in New York. She's now appearing in an off-Broadway production! Isn't that exciting?"

Todd shrugged. "Her mother must be very proud."

Elizabeth sighed. Todd could at least try to act enthusiastic about something that was so important to her. "Well, I can't wait to tell Diane Norton about May," she said. "For years she's been living in the same city as her high-school buddy, and she doesn't even know it."

Todd's eyes were glazing over. "Can't you take a break?" he asked. "All work and no play makes Liz a dull girl."

"All play and no work makes Todd a real jerk!" Elizabeth retorted.

"Cute, Liz," Todd said. "I know you're spending too much time on this silly cheerleader story when you start rhyming your sentences! What's next, pom-poms?"

"*Silly cheerleader story?*" Elizabeth asked, her voice rising. "How can you say that?"

"Elizabeth, you're not researching welfare reform or illiteracy or endangered species. You're researching a bunch of girls who used to jump around, shouting 'Rah-rah-rah, sis-boom-bah!' Don't you think you're taking it way too seriously?"

"Not every story has to be about a deep, heavy topic," Elizabeth countered defensively. "I have a chance of getting my name in a major magazine."

"It's not like you've never been published before," he replied, too loudly. A sophomore who was searching a nearby shelf looked up at them, and Todd lowered his voice. "I just don't see why you have to drop everything else for it."

"No, but you think I should drop everything else for a tuna sandwich."

"I just want to see you!" Todd hissed. "Is that too much to ask? I want to have some fun with my girlfriend."

"You're seeing me now," Elizabeth pointed out. "Does this feel like fun?"

Todd opened his mouth to reply. Then he closed it, shrugged, and stood up. "Let me know when you're finished being a big-time journalist," he said darkly.

Elizabeth watched, annoyed, as he stalked out

of the library. She shook her head. She hated to fight with Todd, but it was his own fault. He was always jealous of whatever new project she was working on. She sighed and turned back to her newspaper. He'd get over it.

After school the next day Jessica caught sight of Brad climbing into a rented, bright red Mustang. *Finally, my chance to talk to him in private,* she thought. Well, the school parking lot wasn't exactly private, she admitted to herself. But at least Heather was nowhere in sight.

"Brad!" she called, trying not to seem too eager as she hurried to the side of his car.

Brad rolled down the window and leaned out. "Well, if it isn't my favorite twin!" he exclaimed. "I haven't seen much of you in the last week." He looked her up and down. "I haven't seen nearly enough of you."

Jessica's whole body tingled under his stare, but she kept her voice cold. "I've been around," she said carefully. *He'd better have an extremely good excuse for leaving me hanging like that,* she told herself.

"I wanted to call you, but I've been tied up with this story about those seventies babes," he explained, shaking his head. He shrugged. "Or ex-babes."

"My sister said she's been tagging along with you and Diane on all your interviews." *Lucky Elizabeth,* she thought, *getting to spend all that time with the hunky photographer.* "So when are you going to pay some attention to the *current* cheerleaders?" She flashed her sexiest smile. "To *one* current cheerleader, in particular."

Brad's eyes twinkled. "This story is about more *mature* women."

"Mature is a nice word for *old*," Jessica scoffed. "Don't you want to show the younger generation in action? It'll sell a lot more magazines!"

"What did you have in mind?" he asked with a lazy, sexy grin.

"How about something like this: 'Once the Girls of Seventy-six were young like us, and now they're withered up and—'"

Brad was laughing. "So you want your picture front and center in *Scoop,* is that it? What'll you give me to make that happen?"

Jessica copied his lazy, sexy grin of a minute earlier. "What did you have in mind?" she asked. "And *when?*"

"How about this evening?" he asked. "I still haven't seen much of this town."

"You're on!" Jessica exclaimed. For his benefit she did a cartwheel as she skipped off across the school lawn toward cheerleading practice. This was going to be an awesome night!

The plastic clock on Nancy Swanson's bedroom wall was shaped like a cat. She could see it in the moonlight from her window—a black cat with a Cheshire grin and rhinestone rims around its eyes.

It chimed midnight, its tail swinging back and forth hypnotically.

Nancy had tried for an hour, but she couldn't sleep. She wrapped her kimono-style robe around her and padded in her bare feet to the living room of the ranch-style house on the outskirts of town. The robe had yellow happy faces all over it. But Nancy didn't feel happy. A headache was throbbing against her temples, as loud as a thousand feet stomping on wooden bleachers.

"Music will help," she said out loud. Music always helped. She flicked on the stereo and placed a record album on the turntable. *Good old-fashioned vinyl*, she thought. *None of these modern compact discs*. This was the way music was meant to be played.

Joan Baez's rich soprano filled the room. "Diamonds and Rust." Nancy settled into her bean-bag chair and closed her eyes. A minute later she began singing along: *"We both know what memories can bring. They bring diamonds and rust."*

But the music was competing inside her head with a cheer that had been pounding in her brain for hours, pounding along with those thousand stomping feet. Pounding ever since she'd attended her first cheerleading practice as adviser, just that afternoon. For her first practice she had decided only to observe, not to try to run the show or even suggest any changes. And she'd loved it. It was everything she'd dreamed of.

101

Everything she remembered. She could hear the girls' voices calling the words.

"Give me an S!" Teenage girls, happy and full of life . . . *"Give me a V!"* Heather, Jessica, Lila . . . *"Give me an H!"* Loretta, Claire, Diane . . .

"No!" she yelled, interrupting Joan Baez. Her headache was getting worse. It was a shooting, wrenching pain now, not just in her temples or at the back of her skull but in the side of her face. The old pain again. She grabbed hold of her jaw with her hand, as if she could squeeze it into submission. "No," she whispered. "This can't be happening again."

Not now. Not when she was the adviser to the cheerleading squad, finally part of the team.

"I need some of that vagueness now; it's all come back too clearly," sang Joan.

Vagueness, the absence of memories. Nancy hadn't thought about . . . it . . . in so many years, had pushed it out of her mind. But now here it was, coming back too clearly. As always, Joan knew what she was talking about. Today's musicians just didn't understand what it was like to be a teenager. To be lonely. To be different.

The pain stabbed through her left cheek again, and Nancy struggled to her feet. "I have to stop it," she cried. "Stop the pain!"

But how? She needed something, she knew. And she knew where she would find it.

Down in the basement.

Chapter 8

Jessica leaned forward and tilted up her face to catch Brad's kiss.

"This has been a wonderful night, Jessica," he told her in a low, husky voice. "I hope I haven't kept you out too late."

Jessica smiled, knowing the nearby streetlight was etching golden streaks in her hair through the windshield. "Yes, it has been great," she agreed, thinking of their starlit tour of Sweet Valley, culminating in a make-out session at Miller's Point. "But it couldn't be that terribly late yet," she added. "Could it?"

Brad laughed. "I forgot you told me that you never wear a watch," he said. "Well, *I* don't think it's that late. And I'm sure *you* won't think it's that late. But your *parents* might think so." He sighed. "It's a few minutes after midnight."

Jessica nodded ruefully. "On a school night too," she said. "I am definitely toast! But as long as I'm already in trouble, a few more minutes won't make any difference. I think I need another kiss."

"Fortification against the parental barrage to come?"

"Exactly," Jessica said. "You are so lucky to be three thousand miles away from your parents. They can be such a pain!"

"Let's see if I can make this worth your parents' wrath," Brad whispered, wrapping his arms around her. He placed his lips against hers, as soft as a breeze, and Jessica felt something melting deep inside her. The kiss intensified, and she thought she was flying.

"So, was that worth getting in trouble for?" Brad asked.

Jessica pretended to consider her answer. "Not quite," she said. "One more will do it, I think. After all, you ignored me for nearly a week! You owe me."

"What can I say?" Brad asked. "I was tied up with working on this cheerleader story. Diane Norton is a slave driver."

Jessica rolled her eyes. "I know exactly what you mean. You should see Heather Mallone when she morphs into Sergeant Cheerleader."

"Heather is the one with all the curly blond hair, right?"

"That's right," Jessica said, stifling a shout of joy. Here she'd been worrying that Brad was spending his spare time with Heather. And all along, he wasn't even sure who Heather was! Even better, now that Jessica and Brad had spent a romantic evening together, it was clear that she was the one he really liked.

Only her short, clingy dress prevented Jessica from turning cartwheels as she ran up the front walk a few minutes later. The handsome photographer was hers at last.

After the last bell on Wednesday, Jessica ran to the school parking lot to grab her pom-poms from the Jeep, where she'd left them that morning. She couldn't believe how perfect her life was. Last night had been so amazing. She could still feel Brad's kisses on her lips. As if that wasn't enough, she'd had incredible luck when she got inside: Her parents had gone out for the evening too. And they weren't home yet! They'd arrived just after Jessica changed out of her minidress. Elizabeth hadn't even blown her cover when she lied and told them she'd been home since before eleven.

Jessica scooped up her pom-poms and turned toward the building, but all she could think of was Brad. The young photographer was her ideal man. He was rich, he was powerful, he was gorgeous. . . . *And he was standing right in front of the door!*

Jessica opened her mouth to call a greeting, but her surge of anticipation turned to sick realization. Brad wasn't alone.

He was with Heather.

Jessica ducked behind the Jeep before either of them saw her. She needed to know exactly what was going on between them.

The white-blond cheerleader was hanging on to Brad's arm in an intimate way. Like a *girlfriend*, Jessica realized with dismay. *No*, she told herself firmly. *Heather's not acting at all like a girlfriend. She's acting like a leech!* Heather's blond head was close to Brad's brunette one, and Jessica's heart sank to her sneakers. "He's going to kiss her!" she whispered. "How could he?"

Suddenly a car horn blared out. A silver Ford Taurus appeared, with Diane Norton at the wheel. Elizabeth was sitting beside her in the passenger's seat. Diane rolled down the window and called to the photographer, "Brad, it's time to go interview Susan Mendel!"

As Jessica watched from behind the Jeep, Brad waved to Heather and jumped into the backseat of the rental car. The Taurus drove away, and Heather disappeared back inside the building.

Jessica bit her lip. Had she really seen what she thought she'd seen? *Maybe I'm imagining things,* she told herself, *reading too much into it.* She tried to analyze the scene objectively. That hadn't really been an embrace between Heather and Brad, she decided. It was more one-sided than that. Heather had been clutching his arm. And maybe Brad never meant to kiss her at all. That could have been one-sided too. Heather had made no secret of her attraction to the tall, handsome photographer. At least they hadn't really kissed.

"It's me he likes," Jessica said aloud, setting off across the parking lot back toward the school and cheerleading practice. "He couldn't possibly have feelings for that mentally challenged barracuda. Especially after our date last night!" She bit her lip again. "Could he?"

Elizabeth followed Diane into the Lady Fit Gym and Studios at the Valley Mall that afternoon. Behind her Brad stopped to take a photograph of the gym's main entrance.

"We'll be interviewing Susan Mendel," Diane told her. "I mean, Susan Mendel-Weinstock now. I spoke to her on the phone yesterday, and she's as thrilled about this article as I am."

"How long has it been since you've seen her?" Elizabeth asked.

Diane shrugged. "I refuse to answer that on the grounds that it may incriminate me." Brad rolled his eyes and folded his long body into a chair in the reception area. "Suffice it to say that I haven't seen any of the girls on the squad in close to twenty years."

Diane gave their names to the receptionist and turned back to Elizabeth. "Susan was a junior in 1976, a year behind me," she said as the receptionist looked up Susan's schedule. "She was always the most athletic girl on the squad.

I'm not surprised to find her running a gym."

The receptionist grinned. "Susan is still as athletic as ever," she said. "She's teaching her advanced aerobics class right now. But it will be over in less than ten minutes, if you'd like to wait here."

Elizabeth began to sit down, but she jumped up again when Diane asked the receptionist if she could interview her while she was waiting. "Oh, Elizabeth, you can hang loose until Susan's ready for us. I just have a couple of general questions for her helper here, about the gym itself. Relax for a few minutes."

Elizabeth sat down across from Brad.

"So it's just you and me, kid," he said.

"For now," she said, keeping all expression out of her voice. She tried to tell herself his teasing was innocent, but she couldn't escape the fact that Brad Cotter grated on her like fingernails on a blackboard.

A group of young women trotted by in jewel-tone spandex. "Ever take an aerobics class?" Brad asked her, leaning forward in his chair. "You'd look really hot in one of those outfits."

"'Looking hot' isn't high on my priority list," she said dryly.

"Why are you so hostile to me, Liz? Other girls think I'm a great catch!"

"If I did catch you, I'd throw you back," Elizabeth replied. "I'm not hostile, but I don't like the way you keep coming on to me."

Brad grinned. "No problem, Liz. Why didn't you just say so?"

Elizabeth's eyes widened. The last thing she expected from Brad was cooperation.

"If you don't like the way I've been coming on to you, I'll have to find a more effective way to do it."

"Why do it at all?" Elizabeth demanded, suddenly feeling tired.

"Because you're one of the most beautiful girls I've ever met," he answered suavely.

"May I remind you that you were out with a different girl last night? One who looks just like me but who *likes* it when you flirt with her? Why don't you save the lines and the meaningful gazes for Jessica?"

Brad shrugged. "Jessica is right: You are uptight. Why do I have to limit myself to one twin or the other? I always say, the more the merrier!"

"That's really warped," Elizabeth told him.

"So what did *you* do last night while Jessica showed me the pleasures of Sweet Valley?" Brad asked. "Out with your own Mr. Wonderful?"

Elizabeth felt her whole body tense up.

"Not everyone feels the need to go on a date every night of the week," she said coolly. "After all, it was a school night."

Outside of classes, Elizabeth hadn't even seen Todd since their fight in the library two days earlier. She was hurt that her boyfriend wasn't more supportive about her efforts to prepare herself for being a professional writer one day. But she knew Todd was angry because he thought she didn't want to make time for him. She missed Todd, but she was sure she was in the right. A major basket-ball tournament was coming up soon. How would Todd feel if Elizabeth resented every afternoon he spent practicing with the team instead of hanging out with her?

Oh, well, they'd gotten through worse arguments than this one. She prayed they could make it up to each other next week, after the *Scoop* article was written and life went back to normal.

A small, black-haired woman bounded out of the studio, interrupting her thoughts. She wore a red warm-up suit with a matching headband, and she seemed to pulse with excitement. "Diane?" she said, her brown eyes opening wide. "I can't believe it! You haven't changed a bit!"

Susan and Diane embraced, and Brad stood up dutifully and began snapping photographs.

"Susan Mendel-Weinstock, this is Brad Cotter, the assistant photographer I mentioned. And this young lady is Elizabeth Wakefield—"

Susan's grin broadened. "You were on the cheerleading squad that took second place at nationals this year!"

"Yes, I was," Elizabeth said, surprised. "You still keep up with cheerleading?"

"Not usually," Susan admitted. "But when I heard Sweet Valley was sending a team to regionals, I made it my business to learn more. There's a picture of your award-winning squad on the wall in my main aerobics studio."

110

"I'm flattered!" Elizabeth said. She liked Susan already. The woman's energy level was dizzying.

"Elizabeth is also a writer," Diane explained. "She's helping me research this story, tracking down the other girls."

"You know that Gail and Kelly are here in town?" Susan asked. "Gail is a manager at Lytton & Brown department store, right here in the mall, and Kelly's at home with—get this—*three kids!*"

"Yes, we've already chatted with both of them," Diane said. "Who would have thought of Kelly as the motherly type?"

"Why don't I show you all around the gym so Elizabeth and Brad will have something to look at while we reminisce shamelessly about the good old days," Susan suggested with a wink at Elizabeth.

"Remember that special halftime skit you and Kelly starred in my senior year?" Diane asked as Susan pushed open the door to the main aerobics studio.

Susan's eyes lit up. *"Laverne and Shirley!"* she exclaimed.

"You got a standing ovation for it."

"What was it like?" Elizabeth asked, taking notes so that Diane could concentrate on the conversation and not have to keep track of any details.

Susan laughed. "You're too young to remember the old *Laverne and Shirley* television show that was on when we were in high school."

"I've seen reruns," Elizabeth informed her politely.

111

"I was the only girl on the squad who was small and had short dark hair," Susan explained. "So I was Shirley, the sweet, quiet one—obviously not a case of typecasting! I wore a bow in my hair and a plaid kilt wrapped around my cheerleading uniform."

"And Kelly embroidered a big cursive *L* on a cardigan so she could be Laverne," Diane continued. "Laverne was the tall, brassy redhead."

"Kelly was also a tall redhead. But she was the quietest, most studious girl on the squad!" Susan said with a laugh.

"She was a scream!" Diane concluded.

Brad rolled his eyes, but Elizabeth was enjoying listening to these women's memories of high school.

"What do you say, Diane?" Susan asked, her round face gleeful. "Do you remember the words?"

Diane shook her head. "Oh, Suze, I don't think I could—"

Susan linked her arm around Diane's and began singing a song that must have been part of the *Laverne and Shirley* skit. In fact, Elizabeth realized, it was the theme song from the television program, all about making dreams come true. After a moment Diane stopped resisting and joined in the singing.

Brad had been looking about as bored as Jessica at a poetry reading. Suddenly he came to life, snapping photos of the two women as they kicked their legs.

"And we'll do it ou-ou-our way!" the former cheerleaders concluded their song, laughing so hard they had to clutch each other to keep from falling.

"Diane, this is a side of you I've never seen before," Brad said. "Wait until the folks back at the office get a look at these photographs!"

"Maybe I should break his camera," Diane mused.

"What about May Eng?" Susan asked after a few minutes. "Have you managed to track her down? I haven't heard a word since college."

"Neither had I," Diane said. "But Elizabeth is a resourceful researcher. I'm still not sure how she managed it, but she located May in New York City."

"You flew three thousand miles to California so you could find a former classmate in your own backyard?" Susan asked.

Diane shrugged. "Go figure," she said. "But get this—May has just opened in a one-woman show off-Broadway!"

"No!" Susan exclaimed.

"I called her last night and interviewed her by phone," Diane said. "And I'm going to see her show as soon as I get back to the city."

"Remember when she was the new girl on the squad?" Susan remarked.

"Hey, that's right!" Diane said. "I had totally forgotten that May wasn't a cheerleader until—what? Halfway through football season?"

Susan shook her head. "I'm not sure. That sounds about right. She replaced that other girl . . . what was her name?"

"I don't remember," Diane mumbled.

"There's another Girl of Seventy-six?" Elizabeth asked. "One I haven't heard about?"

Diane and Susan looked at each other. "Well, she wasn't on the squad anymore by the time we won the state, so she really wasn't considered one of the group everyone started calling 'the Girls of Seventy-six.'"

"She was a junior that year, like me," Susan said. "I remember that, because she was in my homeroom. But she was new to the cheerleading squad that year and kind of shy. I never got a chance to know her well, and then she was off the squad."

Brad was halfheartedly taking photographs of Susan, but Elizabeth knew he already had more than enough. She suspected his camera was really focused on a step-aerobics class in the gym behind Susan—a class full of young, attractive women in bike shorts or leotards.

"Why did that girl stop being a cheerleader?" Elizabeth asked.

"It was so sad," Diane said, staring into the distance. "I can't remember all the details, but she developed a disease, a medical condition of some sort."

"How terrible! Did she ever get better and rejoin the team?" Elizabeth asked.

Susan shook her head. "In fact, as I remember it, she didn't come back to Sweet Valley High at all her senior year. We assumed she was off getting treatments for her illness."

"What kind of illness was it?" Elizabeth asked.

"It was a rare condition that none of us understood at the time," Diane said. "Even the doctors were stumped."

"She was a good cheerleader before she got sick," Susan said. "She was pretty, though not in a drop-dead kind of way like Diane or Claire or May. She was quiet and agreeable, and she loved cheerleading."

"But after she developed that condition," Diane continued, "well, it was obvious to everyone that there was no question of her remaining on the squad."

"Did you stay friends with her after she left the squad?" Elizabeth asked.

Susan sighed. "I'm afraid we weren't terribly nice to that poor girl," she admitted. "I'm sure I don't have to tell you how cruel teenagers can be."

Chapter 9

Lila sighed. It was Wednesday afternoon, the day the cheerleaders usually practiced. But they'd had a special practice just the day before, and another practice had been called for Friday. *This is getting to be a little much*, Lila thought. A major basketball tournament was coming up. And Jessica and Heather had been calling extra practices for it as if they thought Lila and the other cheerleaders had no life! *This is not what I signed up for,* Lila decided.

At least the new cheerleading adviser was turning out to be an asset.

"You girls might as well forget the Ms. Swanson stuff while we're cheering," the adviser told the girls in her quiet, sincere way. "I'm happy to be thought of as another member of the team, not some kind of a teacher. Just call me Nancy."

Lila scrutinized the new adviser. If she wanted

to look like just another cheerleader, she'd need to take more care with her appearance. Nancy wasn't particularly pretty—she was really kind of bland looking, Lila thought. Practically invisible. But with some makeup and some self-confidence, she could be attractive. First, though, she needed some sleep. The dark circles under her eyes made her look even older than she really was.

"I don't want to get fascist on you," Nancy said. "Your two cocaptains do a great job of running your practices. That's what's made you one of the top squads in the whole country."

Jessica and Heather beamed.

"I do have some suggestions for things you might want to try," Nancy continued, picking up a notebook Lila had seen her scribbling in during Tuesday's practice. "I also know some neat cheers I'd love to teach you if you're into it. But all they are is suggestions," Nancy stressed. "This is your squad. I want you girls to make the final decisions."

"What kind of suggestions?" Jessica asked warily.

"For instance, I was watching the Pump It Up cheer yesterday—"

"I choreographed that one," Patty interrupted. "Is there something wrong with it?"

"Absolutely not!" Nancy replied quickly. "It's high-energy, with some impressive moves. I was just thinking about the last bit, where the two girls on the ends—it was Annie and Jade yesterday—turn cartwheels."

Annie and Jade looked at each other.

"As I watched it yesterday, I couldn't help noticing the overall picture you made, as a group. Kind of a tableau in motion." Nancy stopped, blushing. She raised a hand to cover one side of her mouth.

"And what did you decide?" Jessica prodded. "It's OK. We don't mind a suggestion."

Nancy took a deep breath. "I thought the whole arrangement would be a little neater, a little more compact, if Annie and Jade did round offs instead of cartwheels."

Patty's mouth dropped open. "You're right!" she exclaimed. "That *is* better! I don't know why I didn't see it myself."

Nancy turned to Heather and Jessica. "What do you two think?" she asked hesitantly. "It's your squad."

Heather nodded. "I think I see what you mean about the round offs. It's a tiny change, but it might bring the focus in tighter on the whole group."

"It'll be cool!" Jessica said enthusiastically.

"I'm not good at visualizing these things," Annie said. "Can we try it once that way to see what it feels like?"

The girls ran through that cheer and several others. And Lila was impressed with Nancy's gentle direction. She was never obtrusive. In fact, she seldom said anything except for when she was praising their work. But the few times she made a suggestion, it was right on target.

"If you don't mind taking a break now, I have

an announcement," Nancy said after an hour.

The girls walked over to the bleachers, breathing hard from the exertion. "So what's up?" Maria asked when they were all seated.

Suddenly Nancy seemed nervous again, as if she wasn't sure how the cheerleaders would react to her news. "I've picked out new uniforms for the squad," Nancy told the group.

"New uniforms?" Heather asked. "We already *have* uniforms. Several different ones."

Nancy looked at her feet. "I know that," she said timidly. "I didn't mean to replace those, just to supplement them. But if you don't like what I've chosen, I'll pick up the phone today and cancel the order." She pulled out a copy of the latest *Cheer Ahead* catalog, opened it to a particular page, and handed it to Heather.

Heather stared at the photograph for a moment. Then she nodded slowly. "They're not bad," she said. "Not bad at all."

Jessica took the catalog from her. "Not bad? They're totally spiffy! Think of all the attention we'll get in those hip-hugger hot pants!"

"Let me see," Lila said, reaching out a hand for the catalog. "I'm the fashion expert here." She examined the photograph, taking in the long, fringed vests and the supershort, low-riding shorts. "Yes," she said slowly. "I can see it. Retro seventies. It's totally in!"

Maria leaned over her shoulder. "They're great!" she squealed. "We are going to be so cool."

119

"I thought we could tie-dye scarves like this one," Nancy said, pulling a brightly colored strip of fabric from her handbag and demonstrating on Annie, "and tie them around your heads, hippie style."

"Groovy!" Patty said, laughing.

"If you're interested, I know a dance routine I could teach you to go along with the seventies theme," Nancy said. "It's to the song 'Crocodile Rock.'"

"I love it already!" Jessica said.

Lila nodded. Nancy was turning out to be surprisingly cool, despite her mild-mannered librarian disguise. Even Heather was gazing up at her with one of the few genuine, sincere smiles Lila had ever seen from the girl.

Suddenly Lila was looking forward to the extra practices.

Two hours later, Nancy paced the length of the darkened school library, her mind reeling. If only she could turn her brain off, quiet her thoughts. If only she could sleep.

Her pulse was racing. Tension coursed through her body, and a tune coursed through her head: Elton John's "Crocodile Rock." Ever since she'd mentioned the old cheerleading routine to the girls, the song had stuck with her.

She remembered when she used to dance that routine. They'd done it at the very first football game of the season. The crowd went crazy. That was when George first noticed her.

He'd come up to her at the dance that followed the opening game. He'd asked her to dance with him, and they'd swayed in each other's arms all night.

"George!" she whispered, squeezing her eyelids shut to hold back the tears.

That song, that cheer . . . it had been one of her very favorite ones. Until the horror. The pain. "I can't think about it anymore!" she said aloud. She ran to the stereo and flicked it on to the classic rock station. She needed a different song, something that would block out the memories.

Janis Ian's voice filled the room instead. *"I learned the truth at seventeen, that love was meant for beauty queens—"*

"Oh, man!" Nancy whispered. "Not that! Anything but that."

She couldn't fight it anymore. She'd thought she'd finally achieved her dream, become part of the team. She'd thought she finally had her life together and could finally get past the pain and humiliation. But being cheerleading adviser only brought it all back. She was seventeen again. And her life was falling apart.

Janis Ian was singing about girls with ravaged faces staying home on Friday nights while the hometown queens got all the guys. Hometown queens like Loretta and Heather. Like Lila and Diane. Like Jessica and Claire. They were all the same, past and present. Only Nancy was different. A freak in any time.

She'd learned the truth at seventeen too. That's when her life had fallen apart, when her face began acting with a will of its own. First it was just an occasional tic, barely noticeable. Then a twitching muscle on one side of her face, a twitch she couldn't control. Finally the painful, wrenching spasms that struck unexpectedly, that nobody could ignore.

That's when her teammates on the cheerleading squad began pressuring her to leave. They expected her to understand. "How can you be a cheerleader with only half a smile?" asked Lila in that elegant, reasonable voice of hers.

"No!" Nancy said. "Not Lila!" Lila was now. Back then it was elegant, reasonable Diane who'd said it. Diane, whose smile was whole. Loretta's smile was whole too. And Loretta was even meaner: "We're supposed to inspire the crowd, not scare them!"

Nancy didn't need Loretta to tell her. She knew the truth. She was too ugly for the cheerleading squad. What about her boyfriend, George, the first boy who had ever loved her? Was she too ugly for him too? Loretta seemed to think so. But the cheerleading squad and George were her life. Nothing else mattered. She wouldn't give up either one without a fight.

"I'm not going anywhere," George had said. "I'll stick by you, no matter what." She remembered his soft voice as he said it, his warm smile. His shaggy auburn hair touching the neckline of his tie-dyed T-shirt. He told her not to listen to the girls, to ignore their taunts.

"How can I ignore it?" she asked. "How can I pretend it doesn't hurt?"

Tension made her condition worse. And cheerleading practice became the most difficult time of all. She'd thought these girls were her friends, people who had embraced her, who had accepted her as one of them after she'd spent so much of her adolescence alone, in the shadows. But her friends had turned on her. She couldn't believe they could be so mean. They wanted to get rid of her, to sweep her and her ravaged face under the rug like dust, like an inconvenient wad of lint.

Loretta was the worst. She was head cheerleader, but she didn't have the power to kick Nancy off the squad alone, so she'd begun tormenting her, calling her names, saying cruel things. Nancy knew what Loretta wanted. She wanted to make Nancy quit. "But I love cheerleading!" Nancy whispered now to the dim rows of bookshelves. "I don't want to quit!"

She would ignore the cheerleaders' cruelty, as George suggested. "Those girls don't deserve their happiness, their popularity," she whispered. "They deserve to be punished, tortured. They deserve a terrible fate. . . ."

Heather seems awfully happy, Jessica thought on Friday afternoon as the two cocaptains walked from the girls' locker room into the school gym. *Her grin is positively annoying!*

Cheerleading practice was indoors that day as preparation for cheering at the upcoming basketball tournament.

"OK, people!" Heather called in a bossy voice. "Nancy won't be here until a little later, but we can practice these cheers without her just fine."

"It'll be a little harder practicing them without Amy and Jade," Lila pointed out.

"Well, where *are* Amy and Jade?" Jessica asked. "It's not like them to be late for practice." She paused. "Well, it's not like *Jade* to be late."

Normally Heather would be going postal over two tardy cheerleaders. But today she seemed only mildly irritated. "Does anyone know where Amy and Jade are?" Heather asked. When nobody answered, she shrugged. "Oh, well. We'll just have to make do with six of us until they arrive. *If* they arrive."

"What's with Heather?" Maria asked Jessica in a whisper. "Since when is she so laid back about cheerleaders missing the start of practice?"

"Maybe she was abducted by aliens and replaced by a Heather clone," Jessica whispered back. "It's the only thing that could make Heather act like a calm, reasonable person."

"It's Jeffrey," Lila hissed in Jessica's ear. "I bet it's Jeffrey. You know how it is. The love of a good man can turn around even the most hopeless case."

"And we all know Heather is as hopeless as they come," Jessica added.

She didn't care if Heather was seeing Jeffrey—or anyone else, for that matter. All that mattered was that Jessica was seeing Brad. He'd had to work on his story Thursday night. But he still managed to squeeze in a soda at the Dairi Burger with her, right after school. And he'd even called her hours later, just to say good night. Now it was Friday, and they had a real date planned.

Eat your heart out, Heather! she thought triumphantly. Obviously Brad had considered his options and made his choice. And Jessica knew the better woman had won.

"All right, girls!" Heather called, standing in front of the squad as if Jessica wasn't an equal cocaptain. Heather threw back her head and tossed her blond curls over her shoulders. "Let's try the Be Aggressive cheer, with the rap beat I added."

Jessica rolled her eyes but decided the battle wasn't worth fighting.

Heather's voice took on a singsong quality: "Hands on hips, smiles on lips!"

"I think I'm going to be sick," Maria commented. Jessica knew exactly what she meant. Heather's little rhyme was too goofy for words.

"Heather, I assume you mean something along the lines of, 'Assume the position'?" Patty asked.

Heather sighed. "I meant exactly what I said," she explained slowly, as if she were talking to a kindergarten class. *"Hands on hips, smiles on lips!"* she repeated.

"Get a grip, you little drip," Jessica muttered, so low that only Lila could hear her. Her best friend smiled appreciatively.

Suddenly Nancy hurried out of the locker room. "Sorry to interrupt, girls!" she called. "I wanted to be here for the start of practice, but you're obviously getting along fine by yourselves."

"Except that we're missing two cheerleaders," Annie pointed out.

"That's why I stopped by," Nancy said. "Amy and Jade won't be coming to practice today. I sent them on a road trip to White Cliffs to pick up our new cheerleading uniforms."

Maria grimaced. "I'm afraid the timing could be better," she said. "I am flat broke! There's no way I can raise money for a uniform this week."

"Me neither," Jessica agreed. "Unless Lila wants to bankroll me."

Lila laughed. "You're joking, right?"

"Don't worry about the money, girls," Nancy announced. "I found some extra funds in the school activities budget, and I've gotten Mr. Cooper's permission to cover the cost of the uniforms."

"Awesome!" Jessica exclaimed. "Nancy, you're a lifesaver!"

126

"Thanks, Nancy," Annie said fervently. "You're the greatest!"

"You don't have to thank me," Nancy said modestly. "As I always say, What goes around comes around. Rewards and punishments all tend to even out in the end. People eventually get what they deserve."

"Yes, that's certainly true," Jessica said aloud, thinking about Heather and Brad. Heather had tried to steal him away from Jessica. And in return she had to watch while Jessica's relationship with the handsome photographer took off.

"What goes around comes around," Nancy repeated in an unnaturally bright voice. She turned her head and raised a hand to cover her jaw again, as if she was trying to hide something. "What goes around comes around," she repeated again, this time in a low, intense voice that barely carried past Jessica, who was standing beside her.

"But sometimes it takes a long, long time," Nancy whispered.

Chapter 10

"I think you're right about needing to rework your lead paragraph," Elizabeth said, gazing over Maria Slater's shoulder at the story on the computer screen. The girls were working in the *Oracle* office on Friday afternoon. Maria was writing a news article for the *Oracle* while Elizabeth was tracking down Rosalia Martinez, the last missing cheerleader from 1976. But Elizabeth had left her own work behind for a few minutes to help Maria.

"You've got all the important information up front—the main thrust of the PTA meeting and when it took place," Elizabeth said, pointing to the screen. "But the attendance numbers are extraneous since we had about the same number of people as we always get at those meetings. I'd move it further down in the story."

Maria thought for a minute, nodded, and moved the sentence. "You're right," she said. "That was muddling up the first paragraph. It's a lot clearer now. Thanks."

The door opened, and Elizabeth looked up. For a moment she felt as if her heart had stopped. Todd was there, his broad shoulders filling the doorway. As soon as he saw her he tensed up.

"Hey, Todd," Maria sang out. "Are you all ready for the big basketball bash next week?"

"Hey, Maria," he returned. "Yep, Palisades is our only real competition in this tournament. But I think we'll take them. Uh, hi, Liz," he added in an offhand way, as if it was an afterthought.

"Hi," Elizabeth said softly. "Did you want to talk to me about something?"

Todd looked her in the face for the first time in days. Elizabeth's breath caught in her throat. For the thousandth time she realized what a beautiful shade of brown his eyes were. He opened his mouth as if to speak. Then he bit his lip and looked down at his hands.

"Oh!" he said suddenly, holding up a piece of paper as if he'd just noticed that it was in his hand. "I almost forgot what I came here for. The coach asked me to drop this by for John." John Pfeifer was the *Oracle*'s sports editor.

"What is it?" Elizabeth asked, her heart deflating in her chest.

"Just the starting lineups for all the teams in the

first round of the basketball tournament," Todd replied.

Elizabeth nodded. "You can leave it in John's box, over there," she said, pointing.

"Thank you," he said formally. A few seconds later the door was swinging shut behind him.

"Holy Cold Shoulder, Batman!" Maria exclaimed. "If I didn't know better, girl, I'd think you two barely knew each other. Did you have a fight with Todd and forget to tell your closest friends about it?"

"I didn't forget. I just couldn't bear to talk about it," Elizabeth said with a sigh. "Not that I've had much time to talk with you and Enid this week," she added.

"Let me guess, it's the same old argument you and Todd always have: Fill in the name of Liz's current project. Todd's all, like, 'You're spending too much time on that *Scoop* scoop and neglecting me!' And you're all, 'Can't you see how important this is to me? It's only for a few days! Get a life!'"

"You sound exactly like us both," Elizabeth said with a laugh. "But we're not actually fighting anymore. We're just totally polite and totally distant."

"I hadn't noticed," Maria said dryly.

"Don't you think he's being unreasonable, Maria? He knows I love him. Why can't he cut me a little slack now and then when I'm working on a writing project that matters to me? He does this every single time!"

"For the most part I agree with you," Maria said.

"This *Scoop* article has kept you tied up for about as long as his basketball tournament next week will keep him busy. He ought to be able to understand that and to know it's not any reflection on him if you can't devote every waking hour to his entertainment."

"Why do I sense a 'but' in there?" Elizabeth asked warily.

"Face it, Liz. You've got some solid workaholic tendencies. Sometimes you go overboard on your forays into the professional world of publishing."

Elizabeth bit her lip. "*Flair* magazine?"

"Yes, your internship in fashion publishing does come to mind," Maria said. "That was one scary place, girl! And it did some scary things to your mind."

"I did get sort of carried away, didn't I?" Elizabeth admitted. "You know how sorry I am about the way I treated you and Enid."

"We thought we'd lost you for good to all the publishing goddesses in that place, with their long blazers and short skirts—and hair colors not found in nature!"

"But Todd got carried away too," Elizabeth pointed out. While Elizabeth tried desperately to impress *Flair*'s managing editor, Todd had unwittingly impressed the head photographer—and found himself modeling swimwear.

"He did let all that adoration go to his head," Maria agreed, laughing. "But the point is, you're the one who throws herself into every new project, body and soul. Todd's overreacting this time, but his heart's in the right place. He's afraid of losing you to your writing career."

"Todd's not going to lose me," Elizabeth said. "I love him."

"I know that, and you know that. But have you told Todd lately?"

"Maybe not in so many words," Elizabeth admitted. "But I'm still annoyed with him. He knew all along that this was a short-time project. There was no reason to make such a big deal about the fact that I wanted to pay attention to something besides him for a week or so. He can be so . . . *needy.*"

Maria shrugged. "He's a guy, Liz. It goes with the territory. Do you think the current blowup will blow over?"

"I suppose so," Elizabeth said. "We've got a lot of history together. And I really am wrapping up this research on the cheerleaders."

"Did you find the last couple?" Maria asked. "What was that one name? Rosanna? Rosemarie? Roslynn?"

"Rosalia Martinez," Elizabeth answered. "I found a phone number for her, but I tried it, and it's disconnected."

"Some of those former cheerleaders are pretty high-powered," Maria said. "What's this one? A cabinet secretary? A corporate executive? An exotic dancer?"

"Believe it or not, she used to be an L.A. Laker Girl," Elizabeth replied. "I'm not sure what she's doing now, but the disconnected number is in Los

Angeles. I don't know if she's still in southern California."

"How about the other missing cheerleader?" Maria asked. "Any luck with her?"

"I can't locate anyone named Loretta Bari, but I've found a *Gina* Bari in Bridgewater. I'm not certain, but I assume they're related."

"What else do you have to do once you've finished tracking down these people?" Maria asked.

"Compile my notes for Diane, finish up any interviews she wants my help with, and sit back and wait for *Scoop* magazine to come out!"

"With a line of print that reads, 'Research assistance provided by Elizabeth Wakefield,' right?"

Elizabeth grinned. "That does sound good, doesn't it?"

It had taken an hour of groveling, but Jessica had finally convinced Lila to lend her an outfit for her date with Brad on Friday night. She modeled it in front of the full-length mirror in Elizabeth's room.

"What do you think?" she asked her sister, who was sitting at her desk, organizing a stack of file cards with research notes for the *Scoop* article.

Elizabeth turned in her chair. "Stunning," she pronounced. "That shimmery silver is awesome on you!"

Jessica smoothed the satin sheath over her hips. "You don't think it makes me look fat, do you?"

"You can't be serious."

"You're right! I'm not!" Jessica said. She inspected

her shoulders in the mirror. "Do you think it's bare enough on top?"

"If it were any barer, Dad wouldn't let you out of the house."

"Perfect!" Jessica said, smiling at her reflection. "Brad is going to die when he sees me in this dress."

"Is that what people mean when they say someone is *dressed to kill?*" Elizabeth asked wryly.

"Maybe I should wear my hair up," Jessica mused. She twisted it in her hands and held it against her scalp, scrutinizing her reflection from different angles. Then she shook it loose. "No, I'll leave it down. I have a feeling Brad is going to be itching to run his fingers through it."

"Jessica, I don't want to play the big sister—"

"You *always* play the big sister!" Jessica complained. "Your greatest thrill in life is reminding me that you're an entire four minutes older than I am."

"It's just that, well, about Brad—"

"*Don't!*" Jessica ordered. "I know you don't like him, Lizzie. But I don't want to hear about it. *I* like him a lot, and that's what's important."

Elizabeth nodded glumly. "OK, I won't say anything."

"You're a total bummer tonight," Jessica observed, grabbing a silver chain belt from a hook in Elizabeth's closet and draping it experimentally around her waist. "What's putting your enjoyment on pause? I know—you've already finished your homework, so the weekend is stretching out in front of you, utterly devoid of meaning!"

"Did I just hear you use the phrase, 'utterly devoid of meaning'?" Elizabeth asked. "Are you running a fever?"

"Sorry, it just slipped out," Jessica said. "That poetry paper I wrote at the last minute last week must have had a disruptive influence on my coolness factor."

"Your secret is safe with me," Elizabeth assured her.

"Seriously, Lizzie. You don't look like a happy camper. Trouble with Toddy boy?"

"How did you know?"

Jessica shrugged. "It's Friday night, and you're not getting dressed for a date. Are you two having a fight?" At least that would be more interesting than Elizabeth and Todd's usually uneventful relationship, she thought.

"Not exactly a fight," Elizabeth replied. "I've just been so busy with this *Scoop* article. I'd like to go out with Todd tonight, but I have to finish organizing my notes." She waved an arm at her stacks of file cards.

"I can see your dilemma," Jessica said, gesturing with both her hands in turn. "Hunky guy, little piles of paper. Hunky guy, little piles of paper. It's a rough choice."

The phone rang, and Jessica sprang to answer it before Elizabeth could put down her pen.

"Jessica, this is Dyan Sutton, Amy's mother,"

said the familiar voice of the WXAB television sportscaster, sounding a little distorted over the phone. "Amy never came home from school today. Is she with you?"

Jessica shook her head. "No, Ms. Sutton. I haven't seen her since French class. She must still be out at White Cliffs."

"White Cliffs?" Ms. Sutton asked. "What is she doing there?"

Jessica silently cursed Amy for putting her in this position. No doubt her friend had taken advantage of the out-of-town road trip and was out partying somewhere.

"Ms. Swanson, the cheerleading adviser, needed somebody to go pick up our new uniforms," she told her friend's mother. "Amy and Jade Wu went to the outlet in White Cliffs for her."

"Without telling me?" Amy's mother asked.

"Apparently," Jessica said dryly. Elizabeth looked up, curious, and Jessica rolled her eyes. Amy Sutton's whereabouts was not exactly at the top of her priority list for things to think about right now. She still had to make a final decision about the belt, put on her makeup, and select her earrings for her date tonight. Any spare time should be spent thinking about her hunky photographer, not about Amy's worried mom. "Maybe she tried to call you this afternoon, when Ms. Swanson asked her to go, but you weren't home yet."

"If so, she should have left a message on the machine," Amy's mother insisted.

This was getting old, fast. One part of her knew that the woman was just worried about her daughter and not thinking quite straight. But she sounded like she expected Jessica to produce her blond friend out of thin air. *I don't have time for this*, Jessica told herself.

"Look, Ms. Sutton," she said into the receiver. "Jade Wu is one of the nicest, most responsible girls at school. And Amy is an excellent driver." She didn't really know that, but it sounded like something a mother would want to hear. "White Cliffs is quite a drive from here. Maybe the uniforms weren't ready, and they decided to stay overnight rather than drive home after dark."

"Jade Wu, did you say?" Ms. Sutton asked. "I'll give her parents a ring. Maybe she's called them about a change in the girls' plans."

Jessica didn't care who Ms. Sutton called next, as long as she left Jessica alone. "That's a sensible idea," she said in an approving tone. "Of course, I'll let you know if I hear anything from Amy or Jade."

She replaced the receiver and put her hands on her hips. "Parents!" she complained dramatically.

"Amy and Jade are missing?" Elizabeth asked, her forehead wrinkled with worry lines.

Jessica waved her hand dismissively. "Not likely! They probably just found a good party on the way home from the cheerleading outlet."

137

"I can believe that of Amy, but it sure doesn't sound like Jade."

"No, it doesn't," Jessica admitted. "But Jade might not have had any choice. Amy was driving!"

"I guess they'd have called if anything went wrong," Elizabeth said. "You know, if the car broke down or something."

"Sure, they would have," Jessica said. "But I have a much more urgent problem I need your help with."

"What's that?"

"Does the dress look sexier with the belt or without it?"

Nancy sprawled in her beanbag chair on Friday night, the smiley-face robe tied tightly around her waist. There were noises in the basement, and she didn't want to hear them. She climbed out of the mass of squashy vinyl and stomped loudly on the floor. The noises stopped for a few minutes, but then they were back again, as grating as ever.

Another sound hid the bad noises for a moment—the music of the cat-shaped plastic clock in the bedroom. Nancy counted ten chimes. Ten o'clock. That was much better, but only for a minute. When the black cat finished ringing, the noises downstairs were back, as infuriating as before.

"I'll drown them out!" she decided. She lunged

for her stereo and switched it on to her usual station. The Doobie Brothers' song "Black Water" filled the house.

"That's it," she murmured, settling back into the beanbag chair. "Drown out the noises. Drown them in black water," she said. She knew she had to sleep, but it was so hard. Why was everything so hard lately? She snuggled into the cool vinyl haunch of the beanbag chair, wondering whether the noisy girls were snuggling against something warmer.

Moonlight filtered through the macramé curtain that hung across the window above her. *"Mississippi moon, won't you keep on shining on me?"* she pleaded along with the record. She remembered another night when the moon shone, a long time ago. . . .

The moon shone through the back window of Brad's rented Mustang. Jessica knew it was shimmering along the contours of her body in the silver dress. And she'd definitely made the right choice about wearing her hair loose and sexy. One of Brad's hands was entwined in her hair, playing gently with the soft strands in the most deliciously sensuous way Jessica could imagine. His other hand was around her shoulders, holding her close.

For dinner Brad had taken her up the coast to Castillo San Angelo, one of the most romantic restaurants in the area. It was in a sprawling, turn-of-the-century house, built by an eccentric

Spaniard who apparently loved views of the ocean and the sweet smell of honeysuckle.

After dinner they'd walked on the beach and then started the drive back to Sweet Valley. Only somehow they'd ended up at Miller's Point.

Jessica didn't remember if she had suggested the overlook or if he had. All she knew was that Brad's kisses were amazing. They started out slow and gentle and then grew in passion until she thought she would explode. She knew she'd have to use all her self-control to keep from going further than she wanted to. Everything was hotter and heavier than on their previous dates. But kissing Brad was so wonderful that she couldn't get enough of it.

She knew their relationship was based purely on physical attraction, but as she'd told Elizabeth the week before, this was only a fling. Physical attraction was enough. More than enough.

Brad's voice spoke in her ear, as soft and smooth as the moonlight. "Forget about everything else," he told her. "Think only about the two of us. Right here. Right now."

The cat chimed eleven times. In the silence that followed, the girls' voices rose again, just loud enough to be annoying. Then the voices faded, and Nancy heard another voice through the haze of her half dreaming. George's voice.

"Forget about them," he told her. "Forget

about those nasty girls. You're worth all the rest of them put together."

All those noisy, nasty girls. Noisy on the football field. Noisy on the basketball court. Noisy in her basement, but that was different, wasn't it?

That was now.

Those other girls had been noisiest and nastiest when they were off the field, when they had no audience, no crowd of adoring sports fans. In the locker room. At Loretta's and Diane's perfect houses with the coordinated furniture and the stylish, avocado green appliances. At Secca Lake, when the moon shone and the water lapped against the shore, black in the night.

Black water, she remembered, raising her head to gaze around her living room. She had been dreaming—or remembering. She wasn't sure which. But this wasn't the midseventies. She wasn't one of the teenagers. She was sitting in her bean-bag chair, and the teenagers were making noise. As her head cleared she understood why. The Doobie Brothers had stopped singing on her radio. The song playing now was a soft one, too soft to drown out the voices.

She recognized the music: John Denver, "Annie's Song." One of the girls was named Annie. Or was it Kelly? No, Kelly was before. And Annie wasn't here. Not yet.

The girls in the basement were here, and they were noisy again, now that there was no loud

141

music to drown them out. No black water to drown them in.

Nancy struggled to hold the thought. But she felt herself sinking—under layers of lapping water, it seemed. Under layers of sleep. She was reeling in the years, one by one, until she was back in her junior year of high school. The year her life ended.

"Maybe it isn't worth the hurt," George said as they sat on a rock on the shore of Secca Lake, the moon scalloping the black water with gold threads of light. He had thought the girls would have given up by now and accepted her as she was. Nancy had thought so too. But they hadn't. Janis Ian had a new song out, "At Seventeen," and it was playing on the transistor radio Nancy had set up nearby. The song could have been written about Nancy's own life. She had learned the truth at seventeen too. That was when her face had become twisted, strange, and untrustworthy.

"We're really sorry about this, Nancy," Susan Mendel had said in the locker room earlier that day in the fall of 1975. Nancy raised her hand to cover a muscle spasm that racked her jaw. But Susan had seen it, and the petite, athletic black-haired girl couldn't keep the horror and pity out of her eyes. She bent over the laces of a saddle shoe that were already tied—anything to keep from looking directly at Nancy's ravaged, freakish face.

"We have a chance of making it to regionals this

year," Susan quietly reminded her—as if she needed reminding. "I know how much you care about this squad. You wouldn't want to hold us back, would you?"

Susan was the nicest girl on the squad, the most sympathetic. But even *she* wanted Nancy to go away, to stop forcing the rest to think about the cruelty of life, the chance that something terrible could happen at any time—even to a bright young cheerleader with everything to look forward to. Even to a girl just like them.

But Nancy wasn't like them anymore. She was a monstrosity.

She cried into George's soft, warm sweater that moonlit night at Secca Lake. "You think I should give up, quit like they want me to!" she said. "You're ashamed of me, aren't you? You hate my face too."

"No, honey. Of course I don't," he said in his sweet, soothing voice. "I just hate seeing you so tormented. Those girls aren't letting up on you. Maybe you'll be happier if you don't have to spend so much time with them, hearing the nasty things they say. You don't deserve to be treated that way."

She thought about it for weeks, and she decided George was right. She could live without cheerleading, as long as she still had him. She couldn't trust Loretta and the other girls who were supposed to be her friends. She couldn't even trust her own body not to betray her. But she could trust George.

Or so she thought.

It was a month after that night at Secca Lake, and the moon was full once more. She'd driven her father's beat-up Ford Maverick to the Dairi Burger, hoping to find George there, to tell him of her decision to quit the cheerleading squad.

She'd found him, all right. He was in the parking lot with Loretta Bari, standing by her Camaro. The car sparkled, its metallic gold surface reflecting the lights of the restaurant. George's back was to her, but there was no mistaking his identity. As she watched in horror, Loretta wrapped her arms around his shoulders and raised her face to kiss him. And Nancy was almost positive that Loretta had gazed straight at her first, a glare of cold triumph.

"You don't care about George!" Nancy had accused the next morning, confronting Loretta in the girls' locker room at school.

"You're right. I don't," Loretta admitted with a smile. "But he doesn't know that."

"Then why are you stealing him from me?" Nancy demanded, the now familiar pain wrenching the muscles of her face. "Why would you do that? He's all I have!"

"And you can have him back," Loretta had said. "If you do exactly what I say."

Chapter 11

Elizabeth arranged a tomato slice on each half of a bagel, sprinkled the slices with fresh rosemary, and carefully laid a layer of cheddar cheese on top of each. She slid her lunch into the toaster oven and pushed the button.

She turned around to see Jessica padding barefoot into the sunny, Spanish-tiled kitchen, wearing a nightshirt and a dopey smile. "What's for breakfast?" Jessica asked, stretching her arms in a yawn.

"Lunch," Elizabeth said. "Jess, it's twelve-thirty in the afternoon."

"Which afternoon?"

Elizabeth rolled her eyes. "You really are zoning, aren't you? It's Saturday, silly. Your favorite day of the week."

Jessica yawned again. "Oh, yeah," she said. "But this week I've changed my mind. I think Friday is my new favorite day of the week." She stroked her tousled hair. "Or maybe I should say my favorite *night* of the week!"

"Ah, Jessica, you don't know how worried I am to hear you say that," Elizabeth said, pouring herself a glass of cranberry juice. "Especially when you float in here like a helium balloon."

Jessica grabbed Elizabeth's glass of cranberry juice and drank a gulp. "Thanks!" she said with a grin. Elizabeth sighed and poured herself another glass. "Where are the parental units today?" Jessica asked. "The house is awfully quiet."

"It's just me, you, and Prince Albert, watch-dog–school dropout," Elizabeth said. "And as of a few minutes ago, only one of us was awake."

"What about Mom and Dad?"

"I hope they're awake," Elizabeth said. "They went downtown to a garden show."

"Sounds about as exciting as watching the rhododendron grow."

"How did it go last night?" Elizabeth asked, trying to sound neutral.

"I looked terrific!" Jessica bragged. "Brad couldn't take his eyes off me."

"It's not his eyes I'm worried about."

Jessica shrugged. "He couldn't take his *hands* off me either," she said with a grin. "Not that I'm complaining."

"Jessica!"

"Don't worry, Ms. Uptight. We didn't do anything

you wouldn't do—believe it or not. We didn't need to. Brad is the world's most amazing kisser!"

Long ago Elizabeth had stopped counting the number of times Jessica had discovered the world's most amazing kisser. "Jessica, I worry about you going out with him," she said. "I don't want you to get hurt."

"I'm not going to get hurt," Jessica replied, pulling a box of raisin bran from the cupboard. "This is *me*, remember? It's *my* job to break *their* hearts."

"But Brad is bad news, Jessica," Elizabeth insisted. "I wish you'd trust me on this one."

Jessica hooted with laughter. "Trust you? You've wanted to keep me away from him from the start. Just because you don't like him is no reason why I shouldn't!"

Elizabeth wanted to tell her sister everything— that Brad had been coming on to her, Elizabeth, since the day she'd met him. At first she'd assumed it was because he thought she was Jessica. But now they were working together every day, and Brad knew exactly who she was and exactly how little interest she had in him. Still Brad flirted with her incessantly.

Jessica popped a spoonful of cereal into her mouth as she pored over the comics page of the *Sweet Valley News*. Elizabeth watched her speculatively. Telling Jessica the truth about Brad would do no good, she realized. Jessica would think she was making up the whole story just to keep her away from a guy she was attracted to—and that would fan the flames of Jessica's desire. Even if Jessica believed

147

the story, the truth would only hurt her. Elizabeth sighed. She was in a no-win situation.

"You know, Liz," Jessica said, "I think you're being mean about Brad just because you're mad at Todd for ignoring you lately. Face it, you're in a lousy mood."

"Todd is not ignoring me!" Elizabeth protested. "In case you didn't notice, I've been busy with this story for *Scoop*. We haven't had a lot of time to spend together, but that will change soon." Elizabeth crossed her fingers under the table, hoping it was true. At least Maria had reminded her the day before of how much she loved Todd. She would be sure to find the time this weekend to remind him.

"Then you're in a bad mood because of Jeffrey," Jessica guessed. "Does it bother you that he went out with Heather? I did some snooping around, and I can tell you for sure that there's nothing between them. It was a onetime thing."

"No, it's not that either," Elizabeth said. "Of course, I hate to see anyone who's as nice as Jeffrey being burned by a dragon lady like Heather. But I don't have any claims on him."

Jessica's eyes narrowed. "Are you sure you don't like Brad yourself, then? Just a little? You said he was attractive!"

"I also said he was obnoxious!"

"So you're not discouraging me because you're interested in him yourself?"

Elizabeth shuddered. "I'd rather date a live crocodile, covered with army ants!"

"Kinky!"

"Jessica, I'm working with Brad—or trying to. I know what he's like."

"Then you know he's a cool person with a terrific sense of humor."

Elizabeth shook her head. "You know, when I first met Brad and Diane, I thought she was treating him like a kid."

"She does treat him like a kid!" Jessica said. "He complains about her all the time."

"She treats him like a kid because he acts like one!" Elizabeth protested. "He's more concerned with partying than with doing his job. He constantly sneaks off to have fun when he's supposed to be working. He's a screwup!"

Jessica shrugged. "If that's true, it's too bad for you, having to work with him. But I don't have to work with him. And the last time I looked, wanting to have fun was a *good* quality in a date."

"He's selfish and immature! If Diane is a bit of a dictator with him, it's because she has no choice. Someone has to keep him in line if he's going to take the photos she needs for her story."

"How much of his time are you and Diane going to be monopolizing this weekend?" Jessica asked.

"*Monopolizing?*" Elizabeth repeated. "Jessica, Brad is in town only because of this story! It's not like he came to Sweet Valley with the express purpose of meeting you, and then discovered this cheerleader article by accident."

"Yeah, but he's having a lot more fun with me," Jessica said. "So what if he doesn't get photographs of a bunch of middle-aged women! What's *Scoop* gonna do—fire him? They can't! His father is the big cheese!"

Elizabeth shook her head hopelessly. "Do you have plans with Brad for tonight?"

"Nothing definite, but I was thinking of coming up with some, especially after the fantabulous time we had last night. You're not going to make him go take pictures of any more of those old-lady cheerleaders, are you?"

"Not tonight," Elizabeth told her twin. "But we have a meeting scheduled tomorrow with Loretta Bari's sister in Bridgewater."

"Her sister?"

Elizabeth shrugged. "We haven't been able to locate Loretta herself. And Gina Bari wouldn't tell us anything over the phone."

"Whoop-de-do!" Jessica scoffed. "Interviews with a bunch of decrepit cheerleaders who want to relive their glory days."

"They're all successful, well-adjusted adults, Jessica. There's nothing wrong with a nostalgic look back."

"You can't live in the past," Jessica argued. "Brad keeps saying to focus on the here and now, and he is absolutely right. I'm going to have fun in *this* decade."

"What do you have in mind?" Elizabeth asked, grateful that Brad would only be in town a few more days.

"I think I'm going to pay a visit to him at his hotel tonight," Jessica said. "He's staying at that fancy place with all the antiques, the Sweet Valley Inn."

"Does he know you're coming?"

"Nope! It'll be more fun if it's a surprise."

"I don't like the idea of your going to his hotel room."

"Elizabeth, get real. I'm not an idiot."

Elizabeth sighed. "Just keep your head above water, OK?"

"Don't worry, big sis," Jessica assured her. "I can take care of myself."

The black cat chimed four times. *Four o'clock on Saturday afternoon,* Nancy thought as she climbed the steps from the unfinished basement of her house. *Four o'clock and all is not well. But it will be.*

"That's another one down," she said aloud at the top of the stairs, listening to the whimpers from below. "Five more to go."

The first two girls weren't as loud as they'd been the day before, but they still weren't silent either. It might take another day for them to shut up for good. Cheerleaders by nature were noisy girls—they didn't understand the value of silence. But they would learn. One at a time she'd untied the first two girls and taken them to the bathroom, her pistol in her hand. They hadn't even seemed grateful. They didn't seem to understand that this punishment was right.

They didn't know why they deserved it.

One girl, the little one with the almond-shaped eyes, was still weeping softly. She was tied in the far corner of the basement, but Nancy could hear her from the steps. Water amplified sound, she'd read somewhere. The leggy blond had stared daggers at Nancy, and she still shouted an occasional obscenity. That noisy girl hadn't been broken yet, the way they'd all tried to break Nancy. But she would be.

The third girl was shocked and bewildered. She was the newest addition to Nancy's collection of cheerleaders, and she was the worst. Nancy could tell from her thick mane of curls. That hair reminded Nancy of another girl—the noisiest, nastiest girl of all. She looked different now, but this had to be the same girl. It wasn't just the hair. They were both bossy. Both beautiful. Nancy had tied her up in the darkest corner, where there would be no light to shimmer on her white-blond curls.

Nancy listened to the noises below, long enough to be reassured that the girls were frightened—as frightened as she had been when she lost control of her body, when she was first held prisoner by her own face.

The girl with the long legs screamed. Nancy couldn't make out the words. But the shrill, defiant cry hurt—like a burning knife that slashed the side of Nancy's face, scoring it to the bone. Nancy shook her head. She couldn't take any more screams like that. She didn't want to hear the noisy girls. She didn't want to hear their shouts and whimpers, their thumps and cries.

She slammed the basement door shut. It was a good door, a thick, airtight door, left over from the days when this house had been an office of some kind. It did a lot to muffle the girls' noises, but it couldn't shut them out completely. She locked and dead-bolted the door, thinking hard. There had to be a way to silence the voices. She closed her eyes and leaned against the door, wishing she could sleep. She'd hardly slept in days. And the more exhausted she became, the louder the noises grew. The more pervasive. Like a single dripping faucet in an otherwise silent house.

Nancy rubbed her hands on her faded hiphugger jeans, now a darker blue on the bottom, soaking wet up to the patches on the knees. A trickle of water ran from the hem of each leg, but Nancy didn't care. She selected a forty-five rpm record and placed it on the turntable. The music of stringed instruments swelled around her, filling the house, smothering the noise from the noisy girls. Electric Light Orchestra began to sing about an evil woman. And Nancy knew exactly who they meant. An evil young woman with a gold Camaro and a glorious mane of hair the color of moonlight.

Ignoring her wet jeans, Nancy sank into her beanbag chair and remembered.

She'd confronted George the next morning.

She'd blushed, and her facial muscles had cramped until she thought they'd tear her cheek apart. But she had stood her ground.

"I saw you in the parking lot, George!" she accused him. "You were kissing her! You were kissing Heather!"

Nancy sat up straight—or as straight as she could in a beanbag chair. "No!" she corrected her memory as if speaking to a second person. "That's wrong! It couldn't have been Heather."

Heather was part of the now. A noisy girl, crying in the basement. The rest of it all happened a long, long time ago. At seventeen. Nancy's own mind frightened her sometimes. It had involuntary twitches and tugs, just like her face. She couldn't trust it.

"You were kissing Loretta!" she'd screamed at George, tears streaming down her ravaged face. Loretta. That was the name. The head cheerleader. The mean one. The one who was to blame.

"Loretta was kissing me!" George insisted. "I was just humoring her. I thought I could get on her good side and convince her to stop tormenting you. I swear, Nancy, I'm not interested in Loretta! I'm not interested in anyone but you!"

Time tugged at the corners of her mind, and Nancy was seventeen again. She looked into George's eyes, and she knew he deserved a girl who was normal.

"I guess I can't blame you for wanting to kiss

Loretta," she said in a small voice. "You must be aching for a real kiss again." The fear of pain and loss of control, of ugliness and humiliation, made it difficult to get that close. Difficult to be that free and spontaneous.

George blushed. "It's OK, Nancy. I know you'll get better soon. I'll wait for you, as long as it takes."

"Why would you do that?" Nancy asked, confused.

He took her face in his hands and gazed straight at her, even when she felt the corner of her mouth tugging downward. "Because I love you," he said. "I'll help you all I can, but you have to be strong. I know you can do it."

Nancy nodded. "I'll try." The night before, she had decided to quit the cheerleading squad. But after seeing Loretta, she knew she could not. That was what the nasty girls wanted, and she couldn't give in to them. Loretta had threatened to steal George from her if she stayed on the squad. Last night Nancy had believed her. But now that he was here in front of her, his eyes full of love and sympathy, she knew she could trust him to stick by her.

"You're a fool!" Loretta shouted at her that afternoon. "All George needs is a little encouragement from a real woman, and he'll know where it's at! Why would he stay with a horror show like you if he has any other option? Quit the cheerleading squad now, or I'll give him that option!"

"I won't back down!" Nancy had insisted, remembering George's voice as he told her to be strong. "It's not fair for you to make me quit the squad. I'm a good cheerleader, one of the best we've got."

"You're a circus freak!" Loretta taunted her. "And you'll never hold on to him."

Nancy trusted George. She believed what he'd told her. But that night he didn't show up for their date. She raced to his house, arriving just in time to see Loretta's metallic gold Camaro pulling away from the curb. Loretta was at the wheel. And George was sitting in the passenger seat.

Jessica flashed her sexiest smile as the door to Brad's hotel suite swung open.

"Hey, Heath—" Brad sang out. Then his face froze. "I mean—hi, Jessica!"

Jessica put her hands on her hips. "Were you expecting somebody else?"

"Of course not! It's great to see you," Brad said quickly. "Come in! By the way, you look totally hot in that outfit."

Jessica was wearing a baby-doll dress in a blue floral print, with the top few buttons undone to show a provocative edging of lace from the neck of her camisole. She knew she looked hot, but Brad was going to have to work harder than that to make up for his slip.

"You're not getting off that easily," she told him,

156

flouncing into the room. It was a living room, decorated with tasteful, elegant cherry furniture. Through a door she could see a bed with a white ruffled bedspread, trimmed in eyelet lace.

"Aw, Jessica. I'm sorry about how I greeted you," Brad said. "Let's just forget it."

"Not so fast! I want you to admit it. You were waiting for Heather Mallone tonight, weren't you?"

"OK, I was waiting for her!" Brad confessed. "We were supposed to have a date tonight, but she's nearly two hours late."

"Have you been seeing her all along while you were going out with me?"

Brad settled himself into an armchair and motioned Jessica to take the couch. "Yes, I have been seeing her. Is that a problem?"

"*Heather* is a problem!" Jessica said. "That girl has major attitude. She's a total brat!"

"She's not that bad. Besides, the issue here is not Heather's personality."

"Or lack thereof," Jessica added.

Brad smiled in spite of himself. "Look, Jess. I never claimed to be a one-woman man. I'll be leaving California in a few days. When I'm back in New York, what will it matter who else we dated this week? I never expected *you* to stop seeing other people just because I came riding into town."

He has a point, Jessica thought, remembering her night at the Beach Disco with Tim Nelson, the linebacker. "Well, when you put it that way . . . I guess

I'm not exactly the going-steady type myself," she admitted.

Brad jumped up and repositioned himself on the couch beside her. "That's what I thought," he said, slipping an arm around her shoulders. "And did I tell you that you look particularly delicious tonight?"

"Not in those words," Jessica said, leaning in for a kiss.

When it came down to it, Brad was right. It didn't matter if he'd been seeing Heather all week as well as Jessica. Besides, she liked the idea of swooping in and stealing her rival's date. Whatever had delayed Heather, Jessica didn't want her to show up at the inn and steal Brad back. She would have to get him away from there, to a place Heather wouldn't think of looking.

"So can we forget Heather?" Brad asked between kisses.

"Heather who?"

"That's more like it."

"Good! So let's go out somewhere exciting and have a good time," Jessica suggested. "But it had better be *really* good!" she warned him. "No matter who else you've been seeing this week, when you're with me, I want you to be thinking of nobody *but* me!"

"I wouldn't have it any other way."

Chapter 12

Elizabeth's voice echoed in her head. "Keep your head above water. Keep your head above water."

Jessica was treading water, and she tried to keep her head up, like Elizabeth said. But her wet hair was weighing her down. She couldn't stay afloat.

"Climb on my back, Jessica," Lila said, crouching on her hands and knees. She wore the shimmering silver sheath, but the water was ruining it. Jessica climbed, and there was Maria, kneeling on Lila's back and gazing toward the bleachers that rose above the water. Jessica shaded her eyes with her hand, but there was no sun—only the light of the full moon. Brad stood on the bleachers, overlooking the black water. He wore his tight jeans, with a camera around his neck.

It was time for the new dismount. Jessica leaped

159

into the air, higher than Heather's triple-herky combinations. Higher than any cheerleader could fly. Soaring, as free as a bird.

And she landed in Brad's arms, snuggled against the soft, plum-colored silk of his shirt. He kissed her, gently at first. His eyes glimmered in the moonlight. And she kissed him back. Then something began to ring.

It must be the timer on the toaster oven, Jessica decided. Elizabeth's bagel was ready. She tried to ignore the noise and focus on Brad's kisses, his touch. But the ringing was too loud—

Jessica sat up. "What in the world?" she mumbled, dazed from the dream. It had been freaky, all right. But she could still feel Brad's hands on her arms and Brad's lips on the delicate skin of her throat.

Suddenly she knew why she was awake. It was Sunday morning, sunshine was spilling through her window, and the ringing she'd heard was the telephone. She fumbled with the extension by her bed.

"Hello?" she mumbled into the receiver, still half asleep.

"Is this Jessica Wakefield?" asked a woman's voice.

Jessica yawned. "Uh, yeah, this is me."

"This is Heather's mother, Georgia Mallone. By any chance is my daughter there?"

Jessica stared at the receiver in disbelief. There

were so many things wrong with that question that she didn't know where to begin. "No," she said finally, wondering when her eyes were going to focus enough to see the clock. It felt way too early for somebody's mother to be waking her up with a ringing telephone. But there was an awful lot of sunlight pouring in through her window.

"Jessica, I'm concerned about Heather. She went out yesterday afternoon without saying where she was going. And she still hasn't come home."

That seems odd, Jessica thought as the other half of her mind struggled to hang on to her dream of Brad's kisses. *That makes three cheerleaders who are AWOL.*

"Do you have any idea whom she might have been meeting yesterday?" Mrs. Mallone asked.

Jessica shook her head and then remembered that Heather's mother couldn't see her. "Nope," she replied sleepily. "I didn't talk to Heather at all yesterday."

Heather never showed up for her date with Brad, Jessica thought. But she wasn't about to tell Heather's mom that she, Jessica, had stolen her darling daughter's date. When it came right down to it, she couldn't get worked up over Heather's disappearance. Heather was too annoying to be in any real danger, she decided hazily. Besides, without Heather there'd be no competition for Brad's attention.

Speaking of Brad's attention, I'd really like to

get back to my dream, she nearly said aloud. *I was just getting to the sexy part.*

"Do you know anyone who might have seen Heather yesterday?" Mrs. Mallone asked.

Jessica yawned. There had to be a way to appease Heather's mother so she could hang up the phone and go back to sleep. Suddenly an idea popped into her fuzzy brain.

"You know, some of the other cheerleaders drove to White Cliffs this weekend to pick up our new uniforms, and they were delayed. Car trouble or something, I guess."

"And Heather was with them?"

"Well, she didn't go with them originally," Jessica said. "But maybe she drove out to White Cliffs to rescue them." As soon as the words left her mouth Jessica decided that was probably exactly what had happened. It was the only explanation that took into account all three cheerleaders' disappearances.

Besides, it would get Heather's mother off the phone so Jessica could go back to sleep. And to her dreams of Brad.

Elizabeth, Brad, and Diane sat in the well-decorated living room of Gina Bari's home in Bridgewater, a wealthy community fifteen minutes from Sweet Valley.

Gina, a plump brown-haired woman, walked to the tiled fireplace and carefully lifted a framed photograph from the mantel. Elizabeth guessed that Gina was six or seven years younger than the Girls of '76.

Gina handed the photograph to Elizabeth. "This was my sister Loretta," she said. It was a posed graduation portrait of a beautiful teenage girl with a glorious head of blond curls and a quizzical smile. Her creamy shoulders rose from a drape of pearl gray fabric, like Elizabeth had seen in other high-school portraits from that time period.

Brad whistled as he leaned over Elizabeth's shoulder to inspect the photograph. "She's a real knockout!"

"Loretta died a few months after her high-school graduation," Gina said simply.

Elizabeth drew in a sharp breath. Even Brad had the grace to blush.

"I had no idea!" Diane said, her eyes shining with tears. "What happened? Do you mind telling us?"

Gina smiled sadly. "It's all right. It was a long time ago. In a way, I felt as if I'd already lost my sister a year before her death. She was never really the same after the accident the fall of her senior year."

Gina and Diane both fell silent, staring at the plush white carpeting.

"What accident?" Elizabeth asked gently.

"I don't remember the details," Diane said. "That

whole first semester of my senior year blurs together in my mind—what with football season, and SAT scores, and early admission college applications."

"Loretta was involved in all that stuff too—until the accident," Gina said. She pulled off her glasses and wiped them with a tissue before replacing them on her face. "I was only eleven years old, and my sister was like a goddess to me—beautiful and glamorous, with fancy cars and handsome boys." She smiled at Diane. "All of you cheerleaders seemed that way."

"But we all looked up to Loretta too!" Diane said. "She was captain of the cheerleading squad; she had the grooviest car and the hippest wardrobe. She could date any guy she wanted. That's one thing that seemed strange about the accident. The guy she was with was someone most of us had never heard of. I don't even remember his name."

"It was George," Gina said. "His name was George."

"What else do you remember?" Elizabeth asked.

"I was at home when the police drove up with Loretta in the squad car," Gina explained, a single tear rolling down her cheek. "She was pale and crying, and there was blood on her forehead. My sister could hardly talk, but the police told my parents that she drove her car off a bridge."

"Loretta managed to give a statement the

next morning," Diane said. "She told the police that she and George had been arguing, and that he caused the accident by grabbing her arm when she was steering onto the bridge. He died instantly."

"Loretta never said another word about him to anyone, as far as I know," Gina said. "We never learned why he was riding with her or where they were going."

"Police thought she was in shock or something and was never able to recall some of the details about that night," Diane explained.

Elizabeth felt hot tears stinging in her own eyes. She knew exactly how Loretta felt. She herself had been in a terrible accident earlier in the year, on the way home from a school dance. Jessica's boyfriend had been killed that night— sweet, funny Sam Woodruff, only seventeen years old. Elizabeth had been driving the car when they left the dance, but to this day she could remember little of what had happened.

Elizabeth had been cleared of responsibility for that accident. But she would live the rest of her life with the knowledge of Sam's death. Loretta had lived with the same knowledge.

"There was a girl on our front lawn when the police drove up with my sister," Gina said. "I never learned her name, but she seemed to be George's ex-girlfriend, and she was screaming terrible things at Loretta."

Diane stared at her. "How horrible! Why would she do such a thing?"

"She kept screaming that she hated Loretta and that George's death was all Loretta's fault. I got the feeling her accusations upset my sister as deeply as the accident did."

"And you never learned who the girl was?" Brad asked. It was the first time all week that he'd shown any interest in the content of Diane's discussions with her sources.

"This is the first I've heard about her," Diane said.

"She was a juvenile, so the newspapers didn't print that part of the story," Gina explained. "To tell you the truth, I wasn't paying much attention to her that night. I was more concerned about my big sister."

"That's understandable," Elizabeth said.

"But I had nightmares about that girl afterward," Gina told them. "I had them for years. I kept seeing the way her face twisted with hatred when she screamed at my poor sister. It was horrible, like one of those hideous rubber masks."

At noon on Sunday, Jessica stepped around a rack of fluorescent blouses in Lisette's, one of her favorite boutiques at Valley Mall. She reached for the tag on a metallic purple miniskirt that was displayed in the window, hoping it was a size six.

She was startled to see a familiar face looking

in at her through the glass. Annie Whitman waved in recognition. A moment later Annie dodged the fluorescent blouses and joined Jessica near the miniskirts.

"Is it your size?" Annie asked.

"No, it's only a size four," Jessica said. "Do you think I could lose ten pounds by Tuesday?"

Annie giggled. "You don't have ten pounds to lose, Jessica. What happens Tuesday?"

"I have a hot date," she said evasively. "I have to have a positively smashing outfit." Actually that was the day Brad was leaving California, and she wanted to look extra special for their final date. But she was afraid to tell Annie that. Annie idolized Heather, and she might feel obligated to tell Heather that Jessica was seeing him.

"I thought you were broke!" Annie said.

Jessica nodded, a sly grin on her face. "I am. But I'll find a way to get the money before my mother gets her credit card bill."

"I'd never have the nerve." Annie shook her head.

"So what are you shopping for today?" Jessica asked, trying to decide if an olive green miniskirt was too drab.

"It's kind of weird," Annie said. "I was supposed to meet Patty Gilbert and Maria Santelli at the record store an hour ago—"

"Let me guess," Jessica said. "You were there on time, but they never showed."

Annie's eyes opened wide. "How in the world did you know that?"

"Like you said, it's weird. I'm beginning to think there's a black hole hovering over Sweet Valley—a black hole that sucks up cheerleaders."

"Huh?"

"Annie, have you heard anything from Amy and Jade since they left for White Cliffs on Friday afternoon?"

"No! In fact, Jade was supposed to help me work on my Trojan-crunch combination yesterday, but she never came by when she said she would."

"I keep telling myself there's a logical explanation," Jessica said. "For one thing, Jade has the world's most overprotective parents. There's no way she could be gone for two days without them calling every police department in southern California."

"Jade told me her parents were going to San Francisco for the weekend," Annie said. "She was supposed to stay with Melanie Forman—but Melanie hasn't seen her since Friday lunch!"

"Amy's mother called me Friday night to see if I knew where Amy was," Jessica said. "And this morning I got a call from *Heather's mom.*"

"Heather too?" Annie asked, startled. "Jessica, this is getting spooky."

"And now Maria and Patty have vanished. That leaves only you, me, and Lila."

"But what could it be?" Annie asked. "Do you

think they're lying in a ditch somewhere, injured?"

"I don't see how!" Jessica said. "Think about it. They were all in different places, at different times. I mean, I can see how it would be possible that Amy and Jade had car trouble or an accident. And maybe Heather was—I don't know, mugged or something. And something else for Maria and Patty. But they couldn't *all* have met up with horrible emergencies! What are the chances of that?"

"How else do you explain it?"

Jessica shrugged. "I bet it's not a bad thing at all but a good thing."

"What do you mean?"

"It's almost as if there's some secret slumber party that nobody bothered to invite us to," Jessica said. "Or a cheerleading clinic. Or a road trip to Disneyland. You know, something that would make five cheerleaders head off at different times without telling anyone where they were going. Except that I can't figure out why they wouldn't tell anyone."

"A surprise party?" Annie suggested.

"It's not my birthday," Jessica said. "And it's not Lila's. Is yours coming up anytime soon?"

Annie shook her head. "Not even close. Jessica, we've got to figure out where they are."

"Yes, we do! Because I'm beginning to get the idea that they're out there somehow, having a terrific time together, with no parents and no rules. That's one party I want to crash!"

"Loretta was different after the accident that killed George," Gina said.

"She seemed quieter than before," Diane said. "Not as—well, *bossy*." She bit her lip. "I'm sorry, I don't mean any offense."

Gina smiled. "I was her little sister! I knew better than anyone how bossy Loretta could be. But only *before* the accident. Afterward I think she lost her self-confidence."

"She was still a great cheerleader," Diane said. "She led us to the state championship and the national competition."

"I think cheerleading was the only thing that gave her something besides the accident to focus on," Gina said. "She never wanted anyone at school to see how profoundly that night had affected her."

"Affected her how?" Elizabeth asked.

"For one thing, she started drinking too much," Gina said.

Diane's mouth dropped open. "I never even noticed!" she said. "I mean, she did drink that last semester of our senior year. But a lot of kids drank. She maybe had a few more beers at parties than the other girls. But I never saw her lose control."

"She tried like crazy to keep it together in front of all of you," Gina said. "You meant a lot to her. Cheerleading meant a lot to her. But in the end I guess it wasn't enough."

"What do you mean?" Brad asked.

"She managed to hold herself together long enough to go to the state championship, to win that trophy. To go to nationals. And to graduate from high school."

"Graduation night was the last time I saw her," Diane said. "My family moved east a couple days later."

"You never tried to get in touch?" Gina asked.

"I wrote to Loretta a few times that summer, but she never answered," Diane explained. "In the fall I started college at Columbia. I guess I was too busy after that to keep track of my high-school friends on the other end of the country."

"Loretta got worse and worse after graduation," Gina said. "She was drinking all the time—depressed, moody, withdrawn. I know she blamed herself for George's death, despite what she'd said about the way he grabbed her arm. She believed what his ex-girlfriend told her, that it was all her fault."

"Poor Loretta!" Elizabeth said, wiping her eyes. "She must have felt so alone."

"Yes," Gina said sadly. She took a deep breath. "One night in September, just after her nineteenth birthday, she drank most of a fifth of vodka. Then she went swimming in the quarry."

"Oh, no!" Diane whispered.

"Loretta's body was found a few days later," Gina concluded. "She had drowned. It was like she'd willed it on herself for killing that boy."

Chapter 13

Jessica paced in front of the living-room window late on Sunday afternoon, waiting for Lila's lime green sports car to pull up out front. Prince Albert, the golden retriever, nudged her hand. She patted his muzzle.

"Can you believe this, Prince Albert?" she asked him. "I speed all the way home from the mall without buying a thing because Lila promised she'd meet me here. And now she's late! She can be so self-centered and inconsiderate!"

Jessica plopped herself down on the couch, and the dog nestled against her legs. "Brad is only here a couple more days. And now, because of Lila, I don't have the perfect going-away outfit to wear for him."

Even worse, Jessica realized, she was wasting a perfectly good afternoon that she could have been spending with Brad.

Prince Albert barked sympathetically.

"You're right. *Forget* Lila!" Jessica exclaimed. "I'll have more fun with Brad anyway." Brad, Elizabeth, and Diane were interviewing some old cheerleader's sister, but they should be finished by now, Jessica decided. It would be fun to be waiting for him at his door when he got back to the Sweet Valley Inn.

She stepped into the kitchen to grab a diet soda for the road. And she noticed a major obstacle to her plans to see Brad. Her parents. She could see them through the sliding glass door, planting a lemon tree in the backyard. There was no way they'd approve of a date with Brad tonight. Especially one that would be likely to run late. She'd had too many late nights in the past week. And this was a school night.

Jessica stepped outside, followed by the golden retriever. "Guess what?" she asked.

Mrs. Wakefield wiped her forehead with her hand, smudging her face with dirt from her gardening glove. "You've discovered a secret yearning to do yard work?" she said, her blue-green eyes twinkling exactly like Elizabeth's did.

Jessica rolled her own identical eyes. "Right," she said. "And next I plan to move to Iowa and become a potato planter."

"I think that's Idaho," Mr. Wakefield put in.

"Is there a difference?" she asked.

"You got me there!" her father replied with a laugh. He thrust his shovel into the ground and seemed surprised when it actually stayed there.

"What's your news, Jessica?" Mrs. Wakefield asked.

"Amy and Jade finally got back from White Cliffs with our new cheerleading uniforms! Amy says they're awesome."

"I'm glad they're home," said her mother. "I spoke with Dyan Sutton last night, and she was sounding pretty worried."

"I need to go to Maria Santelli's house," Jessica lied.

Mr. Wakefield leaned on his shovel. "I thought you were expecting Lila at any moment."

"Change of plans," Jessica said breezily. "All the cheerleaders are meeting at Maria's to try on the new uniforms."

"I can't wait to see your new uniforms," her mother said. "You'll have to model for us tonight."

"How about tomorrow instead?" she asked. "I might be late tonight. As long as we'll have all the cheerleaders together we're, um, going to have sort of a spur-of-the-moment cheerleading practice."

"Doesn't the regional basketball tournament start in a few days?" Mr. Wakefield asked.

"Uh, yeah!" Jessica said, grateful for his unwitting help in constructing a plausible story. "That's it exactly. We're doing a lot of new routines for the tournament. We need the extra practice."

As Jessica ran back into the house her mother's voice followed her: "Remember, it's a school night!" A minute later Jessica emerged from the front door and zipped down the walkway to the Jeep, parked at the curb. As she unlocked the door an old, classic car came driving up the street, a car she'd never seen before. The black Barracuda pulled to a halt.

Jessica looked up, expecting the driver to be a stranger, asking for directions. And there, in the passenger's side window, was Nancy Swanson.

"Nancy!" Jessica called. "What are you doing here?" Then she noticed something even stranger. Lila was at the wheel of the car, and Annie Whitman was in the backseat.

"Hop in, Jessica!" Nancy said. "We need to talk to you."

The ride home in Diane's rented Taurus was silent. Gina's story had left Elizabeth feeling stunned, as if she'd been beaten up. Tears still glistened in Diane's eyes. Even Brad, in the backseat, hadn't said a word since they'd left Gina's house.

Despite the silence around her, Elizabeth's mind was a noisy whirl. Facts and impressions zoomed past each other at dizzying speeds. And a feeling of foreboding was growing in the back of her head.

Loretta Bari had been out driving with the mysterious George. There was an accident. George had died and then Loretta. May Eng was the new cheerleader. The old cheerleader had a condition. Who was the old cheerleader? Why didn't anyone remember her?

Elizabeth was sure she was missing something. Something important. Maybe a clue she already had at her fingertips, a clue whose significance she was underestimating. She felt as if she were trying to fit together a jigsaw puzzle but had no idea what the completed picture was supposed to look like.

To make matters worse, the Loretta-and-George story hit uncomfortably close to home. As she listened to Gina and Diane tell it, she'd had flashbacks—disconnected images from the night of Sam's death. Headlights glaring . . . the mangled door of the Jeep . . . crimson blood on the blue silk of her gown . . .

Elizabeth turned to the window and blinked back her tears. This was terrible. Dwelling on the past was useless. She had to pull herself together.

What I need is a break from all this, she told herself. A few hours of eating french fries or watching a funny movie or gossiping about trivial things. Todd was absolutely right. All work and no play did make Liz a dull girl. Dull as in *stupid*. She was thinking in circles.

Todd, she thought. *I need Todd*. He was right that she'd been neglecting him, she reflected. Of course, she still wished Todd would try harder to understand how she felt, to understand that her writing wasn't something she did—it was who she was. That opportunities like this project for *Scoop* were rare and valuable. That she could choose to be apart from him for a few days and still love him more than ever.

Well, it's time to make him understand, Elizabeth decided as Diane steered the car onto Calico Drive. She and Todd had to talk—it was that simple. Avoiding each other just wasn't working. She made up her mind to call him right away.

Nancy raised her usually quiet voice. "I said, *get in the car, Jessica!*" she ordered from the window of the Barracuda.

"I can't!" Jessica protested. "I'm supposed to be, um, somewhere else right now."

"But Amy and Jade are back from White Cliffs with the new uniforms," Nancy explained. "The whole squad is coming over to my house to try them on. Most of the girls are there already."

Jessica blinked. Except for the location, it was exactly the same story she'd made up to deceive her parents about her planned evening with Brad. She hadn't expected her lie to be proved true so quickly.

But Jessica didn't want to spend the next few hours discussing cheerleading, hemlines, and nail polish. She wanted to spend it with Brad. She could still feel his kisses from her dream that morning. She was dying to feel the real thing. Of course, she couldn't say so in front of Annie. She might blab everything to Heather. *And the last thing I need is Heather infringing on my date!* Jessica decided.

"I really can't make it," Jessica said. "Sorry, Nancy. I was just on my way somewhere. I'll get my uniform from you at school tomorrow."

Nancy's voice turned menacing. "I think you'd better get into this car now, Claire," the cheerleading adviser warned.

Claire?

"You have to be with the other girls," Nancy said in the same cold voice. "We can't do it without you."

Jessica was bewildered. "What is going on—" Suddenly she noticed Lila's pallor and Annie's enormous eyes. There was something very wrong here. Her friends were terrified.

"Run, Jessica!" Lila screamed.

"She's nuts!" Annie wailed.

"Don't move," Nancy said in a quiet, authoritative voice. Even more authoritative was the pistol she whipped out. She pointed it first at Jessica, but then she grabbed Lila instead.

"Get in the car now, Claire, or your friend dies." She wedged the gun barrel against Lila's temple.

"Why are you doing this?" Jessica asked in a frozen whisper.

"Now!" Nancy barked. "Or I pull the trigger on the Perfect Diane."

"Who's Diane? And who's Claire?" Jessica asked. "Is this some kind of a sick joke?"

"You girls are so noisy!" Nancy complained, pounding her fist on the dashboard with each syllable. "I don't want to hear another word from any of you! No more lies about me! No more!"

The gun was trembling against Lila's temple. Her face was as white as bone. Jessica nodded wordlessly, opened the door, and slid into the back of the car beside Annie.

•　　•　　•

"Todd, this article has gotten superheavy," Elizabeth said into the telephone receiver. "I really need a break. Can we talk?"

"What?" he asked.

"I thought we could meet at Casey's or the Dairi Burger. Or I could come to your house if you'd rather." Elizabeth wiped tears from her eyes. "I want to straighten things out between us, Todd. I can't stand being mad at each other anymore."

"Suddenly, after putting your precious story above everything for a week, *you* need a break," Todd said, his voice bitter. "*You've* decided it's time to straighten things out. *You* don't want to be mad anymore."

"Todd! I want us to make up!" Elizabeth cried.

"So all you have to do is pick up the phone, and you expect me to be sitting here, waiting until *you're* ready to remember that you have a boyfriend!"

"Don't be like this!" she begged. "I'm sorry that I hurt you. I guess I didn't realize how bad I made you feel. But Todd, there were mistakes on both sides. You have to see that!"

"I see that *you're* ready to make up, so it's time!" Todd protested. "What about me? What if *I'm* not ready?"

"The important thing is that someone has made the first move. Why does it matter which one of us picked up the phone?"

"You're taking me for granted, and I don't like it one bit!"

"And you're acting selfish and immature!"

Elizabeth countered. "I called to apologize! I'm trying to say that I love you!"

"Well, you should have thought of that a week ago!"

Elizabeth jumped when the line clicked dead. He'd hung up on her! She took angry swipes at the tears that were trickling down her face.

If Todd isn't ready to make up—well, fine! Elizabeth decided. She wasn't going to sit by the phone waiting for him either. *Maybe Enid would like to see a movie tonight,* she thought, reaching for the phone again.

A stereo upstairs was blasting "Free Bird" loud enough to send ripples scudding across the surface of the water that filled the basement. Unlike the bird Lynyrd Skynyrd was singing about, Jessica and her friends were anything but free. She fought against the ropes that cut into her numb wrists and ankles, but she couldn't budge them.

There was no question about it. The cheerleading adviser had lost it. She was totally insane—or "nuts," as Annie had put it. There was no other explanation. She'd kidnapped the cheerleaders one by one and she'd tied them up in her dim, cold basement.

Now the water was rushing in. It already reached to Jessica's hips, soaking most of her miniskirt. When it rose high enough, the cheerleaders would drown. Jessica wondered how long they had until the water reached their faces, until it poured into their mouths and noses. Until they were dead. Was it hours? Days?

Most of the girls were whimpering or sobbing quietly. Occasionally Patty, Amy, or Maria would pound an elbow against a pipe or let out a yell for help, just in case anyone was around to hear. But nobody ever was.

Jessica's nose was running. Her arms were covered with goose bumps. Even her bones were numb. But Jessica had been tied there only a few hours. Almost everyone else was worse off. Amy and Jade had been prisoners the longest and hadn't eaten in more than forty-eight hours. Jade had hardly said a word since Saturday—it was now Sunday night. Amy was breaking out in hives from a mold allergy, and she didn't have her medication with her.

Heather, tied in the corner where the uneven floor was lowest, was hurting the most. Submerged in deeper water than anyone, Heather was ill. Jessica could see her trembling from across the room.

"If you're thinking up a brilliant plan for getting us out of this," Lila suggested to Jessica in a low, controlled voice, "now would be an awesome time to unveil it."

Jessica had no brilliant plan for freeing herself and her friends. And there was no chance of a rescue from outside either. How could there be? Nobody had the faintest idea where to find them.

Chapter 14

The light in the stairwell switched on. Lila winced. The basement was still dim, but the low-wattage electric bulb was enough to hurt Lila's eyes after hours in darkness.

She stared at Jessica, a few feet away in the waist-deep water. Her best friend's golden hair looked like limp spaghetti, and her heart-shaped face was smudged with grime. Her mascara had run, so she seemed to gaze at the world through big, dark holes.

"Do I look as rotten as you do?" Lila asked, surprised to hear that her own voice was hoarse.

Jessica smiled weakly. "Worse!"

Lila knew the two of them were lucky. Along with Annie, they'd been the last ones kidnapped—they hadn't had to stand in the greasy liquid for as long as the others. The water was lowest on this side of the room. In the far corner of the basement Heather was submerged almost to her chest. Lila and Jessica were closest to the stairwell, where the light had just flicked on. Heather's corner was practically dark.

A heavy door squeaked open upstairs and the ever present music swelled louder, filling the basement with sound. Nancy said the music was to drown out their nasty, noisy voices—*whatever that meant.* Lila was surprised Nancy could even hear their weak sobs from upstairs. But even at the high-school library Nancy liked to listen to music. Always rock and roll, and always from the 1970s.

Lila didn't recognize the song that was playing now, but Jessica grinned and sang along with the chorus, weakly and tunelessly, staring straight at Lila. *"Clowns to the left of me, jokers to the right. Here I am, stuck in the middle with you!"*

Lila chuckled at the lyrics. Leave it to Jessica to find a way to make her laugh, even in a horrendous place like this.

Footsteps sounded on the stairs. Lila braced herself for more of Nancy's raving. She wasn't sure exactly what was going on with the woman, but Nancy seemed to be confusing past and present, blurring today's cheerleaders with the Girls of '76. From what Patty and Maria had told her of Nancy's story and from what she'd heard herself, it seemed that Nancy had known the 1976 state cheerleading champs. Apparently they had dissed her, big time.

Nancy loomed over them on the staircase, casting an eerie shadow on the steps below. She surveyed the flooded basement, reminding Lila of the wizard in the animated version of *The Sorcerer's Apprentice*. She pointed to the far corner of the room, the corner where Heather leaned forward, shivering. Her hair already dragged in the deep, dark water.

"You killed him!" Nancy accused, her soft voice echoing against the water, which distorted and magnified it. "You took him from me, and then you killed him."

"I didn't kill anyone!" Heather choked out, her voice weak and shaky. *She really sounds sick,* Lila thought.

"That's a lie. You always tell lies, Loretta. But I know the truth!" Nancy insisted. Suddenly her voice took on a singsong quality. *"I learned the truth at seventeen."*

"Huh?" Lila asked in a whisper.

"It's from an old song," Annie said from behind Jessica. They were tied back-to-back against the same pillar.

"You told me the story yourself, Loretta," Nancy insisted. "The part you didn't tell the police. Don't you remember? I know what you and George argued about that night!"

Suddenly Nancy pushed her hand against her jaw as she leaned heavily against the banister. In the yellowish electrical glow Lila saw Nancy's face distorting itself, the side of her mouth tugging and twisting as if someone were pulling strings attached to the different muscles.

Annie burst into sobs.

"I sure wish I'd paid more attention when Elizabeth gave me the blah-blah-blah about those ex-cheerleaders she's been researching," Jessica whispered.

Lila nodded. If they knew what Nancy was talking about half the time, they might find a way to gain an advantage.

"Stop it! Stop crying, Kelly!" Nancy yelled, lunging toward Annie. Luckily the girls were out of her reach unless she stepped into the swirling black waters. "You always pretend to be so quiet, so scholarly! But you're as responsible for this as the rest of them! This is your fault too!"

Annie's terrified sobs intensified.

"No, *you* stop it!" Jessica shouted at Nancy, her voice full of outrage. "Who do you think you are, scaring people like that?"

Nancy pointed to Jessica and spoke very quickly. "You're a noisy, noisy girl, Claire Lyons! You were always the loudest on the football field, the one who talked the most, who attracted all the boys! You didn't deserve the attention! You didn't deserve any of it! Not after what you did to me. *Not after what you all did to me!*"

This is getting weirder by the minute, Lila thought.

Nancy gasped and clutched at her cheek as if she could dig it out of her face. She sank to her knees on the steps, her shadow a stumpy, grotesque monster, a deeper shade of black against black stairs and water. She suddenly looked exhausted. She rearranged her legs painfully until she was sitting on the step.

"You were driving your car, Loretta," Nancy said in a soft, anguished voice. "Your beautiful gold Camaro, the most happening car of anyone I knew. You always had the best of everything." She smiled tearfully. "Except for George. I had him, and you wanted to take him from me! Just to show that you could do it."

"What happened in the gold Camaro, Nancy?" Jessica asked gently. "Tell us what happened."

"George grabbed Loretta's arm, and she lost control. She drove off the bridge, and George died! He *died!*" Her voice rose as the skin on her face pulled like taffy. "Loretta has to pay for that! She has to pay!"

"But if George grabbed her arm, then the accident was George's fault, not Loretta's," Jessica reminded her. Jessica shrugged ever so slightly to show Lila she was making this up off the top of her head. "So why blame Loretta for George's death?"

Nancy shook her head. "He did it because he wanted to help me!" she moaned sadly. "Loretta was the worst of the nasty girls, the meanest one.

186

She wanted me off the squad. She said I wasn't pretty anymore." She rose to her feet and screamed across the room at Heather. *"I knew I wasn't pretty! Do you think I didn't know that? But you didn't have to take cheerleading away from me! You didn't have to take George away!"*

"How was George helping you by crashing the car?" Patty asked, taking a cue from Jessica and modulating her voice in gentle, nonthreatening tones.

"Loretta was mean to me. You were all mean to me, but she was the leader. She was the worst. George wanted her to stop!"

"Is that why they argued?" Lila asked.

Nancy nodded. "And that's why he died!" She looked up and smiled unexpectedly. Then she pointed to Heather, and her expression grew bittersweet. "So you see, Loretta? He really did love me, not you! He loved me! And he died because of it!"

She hid her face in her hands and wept, rocking back and forth so that the monster shadow swelled and shrank on the steps.

Most of the girls were crying too, their hot tears mingling with the black water.

"We're not the Girls of Seventy-six!" Amy shouted. "It wasn't us, Nancy! It wasn't us!"

"You are the same girls!" Nancy insisted, rocking back and forth on the stair. "It's always the same girls! The same noisy, nasty girls. The popular girls!

The girls who care only about themselves, about makeup and clothes and boys!"

"Amy is right!" Lila announced in a voice that was full of determination despite its rawness. "Those girls were mean to you, but that wasn't us! That was more than twenty years ago!"

"It's different this time!" Jessica reminded her. "We didn't take cheerleading away from you. *We gave it back to you!*"

Nancy looked up as if she'd been stunned. For a moment there was no sound in the basement but the gurgle of water and an occasional strain of rock music from above. She stood up and began climbing the steps. "You are the same, you are the same," she murmured as she disappeared up the stairs. "I know you are the same."

Jessica heard the door open at the top of the stairwell. A song she didn't recognize erupted into the basement in a blast of guitars. *"Welcome to my nightmare,"* howled the lead singer.

"This is just too bizarre," Jessica said.

Rather than leaving them and shutting the door, Nancy turned around at the top of the steps and came back down. "It's too slow," she said, bewilderment in her rising voice. "It's taking too long. I must speed it up! Don't you understand?" She stood for a moment, watching the rising water. Then she skipped lightly upstairs.

The door thrummed shut behind her and the

stairwell light flicked off. Jessica heard the sound of a key turning in the lock and the sliding, metallic thrust of the dead bolt. Then Nancy was gone.

Jessica had never felt so drained. From the silence of the other girls she imagined they felt the same. *Though maybe* drained *isn't the word I was looking for,* she thought, wishing desperately for dry clothes, a hot meal, and a warm fireplace to curl up in front of.

Late Sunday night Elizabeth flicked on the lamp beside her bed. She couldn't remember the last time she'd felt so restless. It had been a long, lonely evening. Enid had already made plans to have dinner out with her mother, so she'd passed on the movie. Maria Slater had a date, Winston Egbert had to study, and Olivia Davidson had to finish a project for art class.

Then there was Todd. All evening her hand had itched to pick up the telephone and try again. But she couldn't bring herself to dial his number. She'd called to apologize, and he'd hung up on her! The memory of that horrible *click* was still echoing in her brain. She'd assumed his annoyance over the *Scoop* story was a minor squabble that would be forgotten in a few days. Now she was afraid it could split her and Todd forever.

She climbed out of bed and pulled her diary

out of the bottom drawer of her desk. She sat down and began to write:

Sunday night, very late
Dear Diary,
Jessica did an incredibly irresponsible thing tonight—but I wish it were me! Apparently the whole cheerleading squad is doing an all-night bash at Maria Santelli's house. I can't believe the gall of those girls! Not a single one bothered to tell her parents about their little slumber party. For hours the phone rang off the hook here, with all the parents calling to see if Jessica knew where their daughters were. Mom and Dad were livid!

Of course, everyone's parents tried to call the Santelli house once they knew that's where the party was. But Jessica and her friends must have decided not to answer the family's private lines. And don't even bother trying the mayor's phone! All you get is a machine and a lot of menu options for departments in Sweet Valley's town government.

This must be some blowout! Naturally it's taking place when Mr. Santelli and his wife are in Sacramento at a statewide conference for city officials.

After a lot of discussion my parents and the other cheerleaders' parents decided they'd all let the girls stay there for now. But tomorrow all you-know-what will surely break loose! I bet the whole cheerleading squad gets grounded for a month!

Elizabeth set down her diary and stretched out on the bed, staring at the ceiling. She tensed up as the door to the bathroom opened—the bathroom that connected her neat bedroom to Jessica's messy one. For a moment she expected to see Jessica there. Then she laughed. It was only Prince Albert. Normally he slept in Jessica's room, but he must have been lonely tonight until he saw Elizabeth's light.

"It's OK, doggy," she said in a low voice. "You can stay with me just this one time."

She stretched out on the bed again, with Prince Albert lying on the floor beside the bed, where she could stroke his downy fur. "Looks like it's just you and me, kid," she quipped. "Todd was right. All work and no play has made me a very dull girl."

After working so hard on the *Scoop* article— and after the tragic story she'd heard at Gina Bari's house that afternoon—Elizabeth had wanted to put everything serious on hold and have some mindless fun. She wouldn't even care if she got grounded.

She wished she were at the Santellis' huge house—eating nachos, watching videos, and letting Lila or Amy give her a manicure. Or whatever it was that cheerleaders did at slumber parties. "I sure wouldn't mind being in Jessica's bedroom slippers tonight, Prince Albert," she whispered. "I wish I could pull a twin switch right now!"

Jessica, she was sure, was having the time of her life.

Nancy Swanson had gone back upstairs several hours earlier, but Jessica couldn't forget the terrible things she had said. As twisted as the cheerleading adviser had become, Jessica had to admit there was truth in her words: *the popular girls, the girls who care only about themselves, about makeup and clothes and boys.*

"That's me!" Jessica whispered, ashamed of herself. For more than a week everything else in her life had taken a backseat to her fling with Brad. She'd lied to her parents, she'd refused to admit that her sister was really depressed. She'd even lied to Heather's mom and to Amy's. Deep down, Jessica had known all along that her relationship with Brad was fun but meaningless. If she hadn't been so intent on dating him and showing up Heather, all eight of the cheerleaders might be home right now, safe in their own beds—instead of standing in frigid black water that reached to Jessica's chest.

She'd been too preoccupied to consider the possibility that Amy and Jade had been kidnapped. She was their cocaptain. She should have looked out for them. But she'd been too blind, too self-involved.

She hadn't taken Heather's disappearance seriously either. She'd even taken advantage of it as a way to further her relationship with Brad!

When Annie came to her in the mall, worried about Maria and Patty, Jessica had brushed it off. And a few hours later she'd thought more about her own inconvenience than about the whereabouts of her very best friend.

"This is my fault, Lila!" she cried. "All of it is my fault!"

"It's not your fault, Jessica," Lila replied reasonably. "Nobody could have seen that this lady was a reality-challenged zomboid. None of us saw this coming!"

"But I told so many lies, and I ignored all the warning signs . . . ," Jessica said. "I knew cheerleaders were disappearing, one by one. I could have talked to my parents, talked to the police. . . . I could have organized a search! If I had, we might all be safe right now."

"Jessica, it wasn't just you," Annie said. "When Amy and Jade didn't come back Friday night, every one of us should have been on alert."

"But I'm exactly like Nancy said! I am like those girls who were so horrible to her! I was more worried about having a good time with Brad than about anyone's safety!"

"You weren't the only one, Jessica," Heather called weakly from the darker end of the basement. "We all ignored the clues that could have told us something wasn't right. It's not your fault Nancy Swanson is totally whacked-out."

Jessica felt a rush of sympathy toward her rival. "Thanks, Heather, but save your strength. You don't have to use it up on being nice to me. I don't deserve it."

"Yes, you do. I liked the way you spoke up for us a few minutes ago."

Jessica had never thought she would want to apologize to Heather. But nothing seemed more important now. If they made it out of this basement alive, everyone would learn about Jessica's lies anyhow. And if they all drowned in here, well, it wouldn't really matter. It was better to clear her conscience now, when she had the chance. "Heather, I'm sorry I've been such a rat," she said. "I shouldn't have stolen Brad away from you when I knew you wanted him—"

"What?" Heather said. "I thought I stole Brad from you!"

"Do you mean to say that both of you have been seeing that photographer hunk?" Patty asked. "I've got news for you, girls. I saw him laying some industrial-strength kisses on Danielle Alexander after dance class the other day."

"What?" Heather and Jessica exclaimed together. But in Heather's case the word degraded into a hacking cough.

"Heather!" Jessica called. "Are you OK?"

"She's all right," said Jade in a small voice. She

and Amy were tied up closer to Heather than any of the others.

"The water's higher over here," Amy said. "It's already up to Heather's shoulders, and she's getting weaker. She keeps slumping into it."

"Heather, I have an idea," Patty said. "Do you have the use of your fingers?"

"Yes," Heather said weakly. "W-Why?"

"This sounds too shockingly simple to work, but we'll feel like idiots if it comes up later and we never tried," Patty said. "Heather, your hands are tied to the pipe that's supplying us with our indoor swimming pool, right?"

"That's right," Amy said for the weakening Heather. "What do you want her to do?"

"Feel around the pipe and spigot with your hands, Heather. Does it have a shutoff valve?"

"Oh, my gosh!" Annie screamed. "Patty, you're a genius."

Jessica couldn't believe it had never occurred to her to ask. "Does it, Heather?"

Heather twisted and stretched her body to reach as much of the pipe as possible. "No," she said finally. "No valve."

A collective sigh whispered through the room.

"Are you OK, Jade?" Lila asked. "You've been so quiet."

"I don't know what to say," Jade admitted. "I was just thinking about my parents, wondering if I'll see them again."

"Don't give up, Jade," Jessica assured her. But tiny little Jade was in more immediate danger than most of the girls. The water was approaching her chin. "Don't *anyone* give up! We'll find a way out of this."

"Absolutely!" Heather said, her voice growing weaker by the minute. "Now that your cocaptains have bonded, the best cheerleading squad in the state of California can't lose!"

"Yeah, team!" Jessica shouted.

The stairwell light flicked on again, and Lila held her breath. The door opened with another blast of rock music. And Nancy stepped slowly down the stairs.

"You noisy girls are too loud!" she told them. "You talk down here, and you talk in my head the way you talked those other times, and *I can't stand the noise!*" On the last five words she rolled a hand into a fist and beat it against the railing. Suddenly half of her face twisted grotesquely, and Nancy collapsed onto the stairs as if she'd been hit.

"Are you all right?" Maria asked.

"No talking, Susan!" Nancy yelled, struggling to her feet. *"No more talking, anybody!"*

She took a deep breath, looked down at her flare-leg jeans, and stepped gingerly into the black water, holding some sort of fringed purse higher than the water level.

Lila bit her lip. *What is Nancy planning to do?*

"I can't have so much talking down here!" Nancy said, her head pivoting back and forth in an unnatural way as she waded through the water toward Jessica. "I have to keep you girls quiet once and for all!"

When she was standing beside Jessica, the assistant librarian reached into the fringed purse. In its side Lila could clearly see a suspicious bulge. She remembered the gun Nancy had held on her in the car when she'd forced Jessica to join them. That gun was just about the right size to make a bulge like that in the side of the bag.

Lila felt dizzy. *She's going to shoot us all!* she told herself in horror and disbelief. *And she's beginning with Jessica.*

"No!" Lila screamed.

Annie began to cry.

Chapter 15

Nancy stood in water that had reached a few inches above her waist, looking down at a girl who was a little shorter than she was. A girl who stood against a pillar in water that lapped at the low neckline of her tank top. It was Claire, and she was quiet now. Nancy knew it was a trick. As soon as Nancy had gone upstairs the last time these girls had been noisy again, and Claire was behind it. Strawberry blond Claire was always behind it—the kind of girl who always had a plan, even if her plans sometimes backfired. Claire talked too much, and she made the other ones talk.

Nancy had turned the stereo volume way up, but she couldn't block out the noise of their talking. So now she would stop the talking another way.

Claire's hair didn't look strawberry blond in this light. It looked more like dirty gold. And her face was heart shaped instead of round. But it was Claire, all right. She couldn't fool Nancy.

Nancy reached into the fringed bag she held above the water level. "I have to do this, Claire," she said. "I know you understand. I have to make sure you'll be quiet." After all, Nancy had to leave the house to go to school. She couldn't risk having these nasty, noisy girls get rowdy and attract attention while she was gone.

"*I am not Claire!*" the girl said in a tight, angry voice. "My name is Jessica, and this isn't the 1970s!"

Nancy's hand fumbled around in the bag.

"Please, no!" screamed Diane, the most elegant girl at school. "Don't do it!" Nancy turned to scrutinize her. She didn't look elegant now.

"I said *no talking!*" Nancy ordered, but this time she stayed calm. She'd found a solution to the noise problem, a way to make them all shut up. All she had to do was put it into effect.

She pulled a handkerchief from the fringed bag and tied it tightly around Claire's mouth. Diane slumped forward curiously, making a noise that sounded like something between laughter and crying.

"What is it, Lila?" asked Rosalia from the corner, her long, beautiful legs deep underwater. Nancy had envied her those legs. Dancer's legs. "What is she doing to Jessica?" Rosalia demanded to know.

"It's OK, Amy!" Diane called out. "It's OK,

199

everyone! It's only a handkerchief. Nancy wants to cover our mouths, that's all!"

Nancy glared at her, and Diane snapped her mouth shut. "You're next," Nancy said.

Nancy felt strangely serene. She'd found a way to make them quiet, to stop at least some of the noises that filled her head and left no room for anything else.

She'd also found a way to hurry the water. Her plan was taking too long. It was making her nervous. So she'd studied her options. And she'd made a discovery—the house had a sprinkler system in case of fires. It was installed long ago, when offices were here, and the sprinklers were still working. In a few minutes Nancy would turn it on, and the water would pour in faster, swirling higher and higher around the nasty, noisy girls.

She felt no twitches now. Her headache was gone. "I can do this," she whispered. "I will win this game. Victory is mine."

She slogged through the rising water, fitting a gag over each cheerleader's mouth. Then she mounted the stairs and left behind nasty girls, darkness, and black, black water.

Elizabeth turned away from her locker at the beginning of her lunch period on Monday. "Sara!" she called, seeing dark-haired Sara Eastbourne hobble by on her crutches. Elizabeth fell into step beside her. "I'm glad I ran into you. I suppose you heard about the Revenge of the Cheerleaders last night."

Sara laughed. "Who hasn't? I heard they were at Maria's house, partying it up all night, without even telling their parents."

"And not a single one of them showed up for school today!" Elizabeth said. "My sister included! You know, last night I actually wished I were at Maria's with them. I bet it was a blast!"

"You don't think so anymore?" Sara asked.

"I think they went too far when they decided to blow off school today. If it were just last night, I'm sure the parents would have been willing to plea bargain—bust them down to a harmless prank."

"After skipping school today, there's no way they're getting off easy," Sara said.

"I thought since you're technically a member of the cheerleading squad, you might know what was going on in those 'pom-poms for brains' heads of theirs!"

"It's all that hair spray," Sara explained. "It weighs heavily on the cerebral cortex."

Elizabeth laughed. "So they didn't say anything to you about this?"

"Sorry, Liz. I probably know less about it than you do."

A few minutes later Elizabeth pulled open the door to the library. She jumped back, startled. Ms. Swanson had pushed it open from the inside at the same time. The assistant librarian fell forward against Elizabeth and then blushed furiously, turning away to hide her embarrassment.

"Sorry, Ms. Swanson," Elizabeth said. "Maybe you need a traffic light at this intersection."

"It's all right," the woman said, taking a deep breath. "I'm mellow with it."

What an odd thing to say! Elizabeth thought, gazing at her curiously.

"Well, I'll let you continue to the library now," Ms. Swanson said. "I was just on my way to the faculty lounge for lunch."

"Actually it's you I wanted to talk to, if you can spare a minute," Elizabeth told her. "As far as I can tell, not a single cheerleader showed up for school today."

"That's what the absentee list from the front office showed," Ms. Swanson replied.

"I know they love having you as their adviser. I thought maybe they'd confided in you about their thought processes on this one. I know they supposedly had a radical time last night. But it seems strange that not a single girl would drag herself to school afterward!"

"Maybe you weren't a cheerleader long enough to experience it, Elizabeth, but there's a strong group identity on a squad like that. If the, uh, *brasher* girls on the squad wanted to declare today a cheerleader skip day, I've no doubt that all eight girls would stay out of school despite tests, homework assignments, and overdue library books. They have a lot of loyalty to one another."

Tension flashed in the adviser's eyes, and she looked as if she were about to say something quite different. She bit her lip instead.

"So you don't know if they're planning on coming in at all today," Elizabeth said.

"Oh, I'm quite sure they are," Ms. Swanson replied. "But not for school. We're rehearsing a new cheer in practice today. The music is 'Crocodile Rock,' and they really dig it. I'm certain they'll all show up for cheerleading practice today."

"Great! Thanks, Ms. Swanson!" She hoped the cheerleading adviser's prediction turned out to be accurate. For Jessica's sake, Elizabeth wanted to confront her about the incident before the twins' parents did.

As long as she was thinking about cheerleaders, Elizabeth decided this would be a good time to solve the last remaining mysteries about the Girls of '76.

A few minutes later she was sitting at a table in the library, thumbing through the now familiar 1976 yearbook. She and Diane had managed to locate all but one of the members of the 1976 squad. They'd interviewed almost everyone, and Diane would talk to May Eng in New York this week.

"May Eng," Elizabeth repeated out loud. "The new girl."

So who was the *old* girl? That was one of the questions still left unanswered by Elizabeth's research. And none of the women they'd interviewed could remember much about her at all. Or didn't *want* to remember. When it came to the girl with the mysterious medical condition, they all clammed up.

She turned to the only photograph she'd been able to find of the cheerleader who left the squad in the fall of 1975. It was a group photo, taken at the first football game of the season. The girl Elizabeth couldn't identify was turned mostly away from the camera. But she thought the girl looked vaguely familiar.

Suddenly somebody grabbed Elizabeth, and a pair of hands covered her eyes.

"Hey!" she yelled, "who do you think you—" Then she laughed with relief. "Todd!" she squealed, throwing her arms around him.

"Does this friendly reception mean you forgive me for hanging up on you yesterday?"

"Well, I'm still a little miffed," Elizabeth admitted. "But I guess I'll get over it."

"I know I was rude," Todd said. "You called to apologize, and I was a jerk about it. My problem was that I really *was* just waiting for you to call! When I realized that, I felt like a pathetic little wimp! That's why I was so mean to you. It was myself I was mad at."

"Does this mean we can kiss and make up?" Elizabeth asked.

"On one condition," Todd said with a grin.

"Name it."

"Put down those silly yearbooks and spend the rest of the lunch period with me. Doing absolutely nothing constructive!"

"That is the best offer I've had in ages," Elizabeth said. She slammed the yearbook shut and reshelved it. Then Todd took her arm in his and headed out of the library, toward the school courtyard with its green grass and sunshine.

"I've worked my gag free!" Jessica called to the dark, wet room. Water was still pouring into the basement through the pipe near Heather. But for the last few hours a sprinkler system had been showering them from above as well. It was like going swimming in the rain—while tied to the bottom of the ocean. "How is everyone else? Who else can talk?"

"I just got mine off too!" Amy called, her voice faint with hunger and fatigue.

"Are you OK?"

"The itching is driving me insane!" Amy said. "If these hives get any worse, you may have another Nancy Swanson on your hands. But I'm more worried about Heather and Jade."

"I—I—I c-can talk, Jessica," Heather stammered.

"Don't try!" Amy told her. "Jess, I think Heather's running a high fever. She's shivering one minute and sweating the next. And even in this light her skin is so pale, it glows."

205

"And Jade?"

"I'm not sick or anything," came the sophomore's voice. "I'm just—" She stopped, choking. "I'm too short for this!"

"The water is awful deep over here," Amy said. "Jade gets slapped with a mouthful of it every few minutes."

"My hands are free, but I'm having trouble un-tying my feet," Jade said. "They're loose enough so I can kind of jump up a few inches. That's the only way I can breathe now."

Nearer to Jessica, Annie's mouth was still covered, but Jessica could see the horror in her eyes over Jade's and Heather's predicaments.

"Keep trying, Jade. You can do it!" Jessica said.

"I get dizzy sometimes," Jade admitted. "What is it now, Monday afternoon? Amy and I haven't eaten since lunch on Friday."

"Don't remind me!" Amy said. "And to think I passed up a big cheeseburger and french fries because the yogurt and fruit plate looked healthier!" she complained.

"M-My fault," Heather croaked out. "Ch-Cheerleading diet." When Heather had first joined the squad, she'd harangued the other girls about their fat intake and insisted on changing their eating habits.

"I'll tell you what, Heather," Amy proposed. "When we get outta here, we're going to the Dairi

Burger for a high-fat, high-cholesterol calorie fest. And you're paying!"

"Y-You're on," Heather said, coughing again.

"Heather?" Maria asked faintly. "You sound terrible."

"Don't answer, Heather," Amy said. "Keep your mouth shut. Breathe through your nose."

"Keep working on your ropes, everyone!" Jessica yelled. "If you can loosen those ropes, you might be able to raise yourself up higher."

"Yuck!" came another voice. Jessica turned to see Lila spitting out what was left of her gag.

"Are you OK, Li?"

"Just totally grossed out," Lila said, stretching her lips as if she were trying them out for the first time. "Now I know why they call those things 'gags.' I can't believe that witch put *polyester* in my mouth!"

"Lila Fowler, you are unbelievable!" came Patty's breathless voice.

"Is there a single thing about this situation that *is* believable?" Jessica asked. "I mean, the entire Sweet Valley High cheerleading squad has spent a whole weekend together—without a single blow-dryer!"

"Jess, if you locate a blow-dryer, please keep it out of the water," Jade said. "If I get to choose, I prefer death by drowning over electrocution." She coughed violently but then continued. "I burn easily."

"I choose death by old age!" Jessica said.

"I'll take death by chocolate," Patty said.

"Is this what they call gallows humor?" Amy asked.

"It's what they call *weak* humor," Lila replied.

Jessica took a deep breath. "This is good, Lila," she whispered. "As long as people are talking and making stupid jokes, they're not going to give up. Help me keep them going until we can get out of here."

Lila kept her voice low. "Get out of here how?"

"I haven't figured that part out yet," Jessica admitted.

"Heather!" Amy screamed. "Oh, gosh, she can't breathe!"

Jessica heard sputtering on the other side of the room. She could barely make out Heather's head in the darkness, slumping forward into the water.

"Stay with us, Heather!" she called out. "Stay conscious! Concentrate on keeping your nose and mouth above the waterline. Don't worry about anything else. Just focus on that!"

"It's like the way you visualize a cheerleading jump before you try it," Amy said. "Concentrate."

"I—I'm OK," Heather choked out. "Thanks, everyone."

"Stay alert and help each other, guys!" Jessica ordered. "Remember, we're all in this together!"

She caught Lila's eye, and her best friend shook her head slightly. Jessica knew exactly what she was thinking. *If we don't think of something soon, we'll all die in this together.*

Chapter 16

Jessica's hands had been free for some time. The feet were harder. Freeing her ankles meant diving repeatedly into the murky, chin-deep water to untie the wet cords. Finally the last knot gave way. Jessica pushed off from the bottom and swam as fast as she could to Heather's corner of the basement.

"Heather! Jade!" she cried. "Can you hear me?" She hadn't heard a word from either girl in at least twenty minutes. "Heather?"

"Jess!"

Jade's feet were still tied, but she'd managed to wrench the looped rope up the pole she was tied to so she was no longer standing on the floor. Even so, she could barely keep her nose above the surface. "I'm fine for now!" she gasped. "Help Heather!"

Something round and pale seemed to be floating in the dark water. It was the top of Heather's head.

Jessica took the girl in her arms and lifted her head out of the water. Heather coughed. "I'm OK," she whispered. "Wrists and ankles are free." But her skin was hot, despite the cold water that shriveled her fingers and made her shiver. Heather needed more than a ropes expert. She needed a doctor.

Suddenly Maria was swimming alongside Jessica. "I'm free too," she said. "I'll get Jade."

One by one the cheerleaders were untying their ropes or slipping out of them, helping each other as much as possible. Jessica felt relieved, but she knew they weren't safe yet. The water was rising rapidly. And the door at the top of the steps was airtight, with a dead bolt.

Elizabeth leaned against the wall by the school entrance after school on Monday, waiting for Todd to finish with basketball practice. She got a warm, peaceful feeling every time she thought about how they'd finally made up. Now they were as much in love as ever.

A black Barracuda, a real classic, cruised through the parking lot. Elizabeth recognized Nancy Swanson at the wheel and waved. "What happened with cheerleading practice?" she called out. "Did Jessica and the other girls show up?"

Ms. Swanson nodded. Then she gave a special cheerleading-style wave of her arm, yelled, "Go, Gladiators!" and drove away.

Elizabeth laughed. She'd been right about this cheerleader business being a way to build confidence for the timid library assistant. Suddenly she was acting as if she'd been a cheerleader all her life.

All her life . . .

Elizabeth froze. "No," she whispered. "It couldn't be." She took a deep breath and tried to visualize a photograph in the 1976 yearbook, the picture of the cheerleaders at the first football game of the season. There was one cheerleader who had turned away from the camera. A cheerleader who didn't appear in any of the other photographs. A cheerleader identified only as the girl May Eng had replaced on the squad. A cheerleader with some sort of medical condition or disease.

Elizabeth conjured up the image of the photograph in her mind. She'd certainly looked at it often enough. This time she knew exactly who the mystery cheerleader was. It was Nancy Swanson!

"Why didn't she tell me?" Elizabeth whispered. "Why did she keep brushing me away from the topic?"

A vague feeling of foreboding had been bothering Elizabeth since she'd heard the story of Loretta Bari. Now she was gripped by a shocked sense of dread. Something wasn't right. Elizabeth still didn't know how the pieces fit together. But she knew that something was terribly, horribly wrong.

"I have to talk to Nancy!" she said suddenly, fumbling in her purse for the keys to the Jeep. She wasn't sure why, but she knew it was important. Todd would just have to understand.

*   *   *

Jessica and the other girls huddled on the top few stairs, clutching each other for warmth and moral support.

They'd pounded their fists on the thick, heavy door. They'd tried to pick the lock with a sliver of metal from the barrette Maria had been wearing in her hair. They'd screamed and pleaded through the door, but they'd received no reply.

The water had reached the basement ceiling now, and it was still rising in the stairwell. This time there was nowhere else to go.

Elizabeth rapped on Ms. Swanson's front door. But there was music playing inside—loud rock-and-roll music. She doubted the cheerleading adviser could hear her. "Ms. Swanson!" she yelled at the door. "It's Elizabeth Wakefield!"

The door was wrenched open, and Nancy Swanson stood in the doorway, her eyes wide and blank. She bit her lip. "Elizabeth," she said, stepping out onto the front porch and closing the door behind her. "What can I do for you?"

"Why didn't you tell me you were a cheerleader with the Girls of Seventy-six?" Elizabeth demanded, taking a seat. "You knew about my research!"

Ms. Swanson opened her mouth but couldn't seem to get any words out. As Elizabeth watched, one side of her face began to twitch sporadically. Elizabeth tried not to avert her eyes, but she was getting the feeling that she'd see much worse before long. She was sure she'd just jumped into something much bigger and more complicated than she could have imagined.

"What's that noise?" she asked.

The cheerleading adviser shook her head frantically. "I don't hear any noise. There is no more noise," she said, giving each syllable equal weight, like gunshots. "I made the noise stop."

"What do you mean?" Elizabeth asked, horrified. She'd never seen Ms. Swanson act so strangely.

The expression on the woman's face modulated into something more normal. The tic seemed to have passed. "Sorry," she said. "I'm not making a lot of sense today. I guess I haven't been sleeping well. I'm afraid I don't react well under stress."

"I still hear odd noises," Elizabeth said. "Whooshing and gurgling sounds."

"Plumbing problems," Ms. Swanson explained abruptly.

"I'd like you to be honest with me about the cheerleaders," Elizabeth said. "Did—"

A phone rang inside, and the cheerleading adviser jumped to her feet. "Wait here."

Ms. Swanson closed the screen door but left the regular door open. So Elizabeth sidled close to the door to see if she could hear what was happening inside.

"The girls?" Ms. Swanson asked her caller. "I don't know. Missing?"

At the word *missing* Elizabeth felt a stab of fear. And suddenly her overwhelming sense of foreboding came into focus. And its focal point was Jessica. Often she could feel when Jessica was in danger. That wasn't unusual among identical twins, she knew. And right now her twin-sister vibes were shrieking warnings.

"For uniforms?" Ms. Swanson asked. "No, I didn't authorize that. They already have perfectly good uniforms. . . . What do you mean, they weren't at the mayor's house last night?"

Elizabeth's hand flew to her mouth. Had the cheerleaders' night out been a smoke screen for something else? she wondered. If so, *where was Jessica?*

"This is all very distressing," Ms. Swanson said, but she didn't look distressed. "Please let me know if you hear anything."

Elizabeth tried to piece together the story. Jessica and her squad weren't on a two-day party binge. They were missing. Gone. In danger. Nancy was acting normal one minute and like a maniac the next. Her face was twisting and contorting in horrifying ways.

She remembered Diane and Susan talking about the cheerleader who left the squad during football season. The girls had been cruel to her. It sounded as if she might have had some kind of breakdown.

A muffled scream sounded from inside the house, followed by a thump. Elizabeth ran inside. She had to find Jessica and the others. She nearly skidded on a puddle of water on the floor.

Ms. Swanson was hanging up the telephone as Elizabeth burst into the living room. "Where are they?" Elizabeth demanded.

"Where are what?"

"The cheerleaders!" Elizabeth yelled. "They never showed up for practice today, did they? They didn't have a slumber party last night, and they never went to White Cliffs for new uniforms. *What have you done with them?*"

The woman's jaw twitched dramatically. *No wonder she covers her mouth when she smiles,* Elizabeth thought.

"I didn't do anything to them! It was all their fault. Especially Loretta's."

"Loretta Bari?"

"They were nasty, all of them! That's how their type is. They care only about looks. They'll steal your boyfriend, steal your life!" She was shouting now. "They deserve their punishment!"

"What punishment?" Elizabeth asked, trying to squelch the horror in her voice so Ms. Swanson would keep talking.

The woman was crying. "They had no right to do that to me! Those nasty, noisy girls."

Elizabeth heard a loud thud followed by a splash. "What's that?"

"That's nothing!" Ms. Swanson insisted. "I fixed the problem. It will be over much quicker now, and not so noisy."

Elizabeth ran from the room, and Ms. Swanson followed. A heavy door in the hallway probably led to a basement. It had a lock and a dead bolt. And she could hear somebody pounding on it from the other side.

Elizabeth threw herself against the door and slid open the dead bolt. "Jessica!" she screamed. "Are you in there?" But the other lock wouldn't budge without a key.

"Lizzie!" Jessica's voice came muffled through the door. "All eight of us are in here!"

From the corner of her eye Elizabeth saw Ms. Swanson whip a handgun out from under her jacket. Before she had time to aim, Elizabeth's hand closed on the nearest heavy object—some sort of sculpture or statuette. She swung it against the ex-cheerleader's gun with every ounce of strength she could summon. But it wasn't enough.

Ms. Swanson managed to hold on to the pistol and recovered quickly. "Don't make me shoot you," she warned, her gun trained on Elizabeth. "You aren't one of them! You weren't supposed to be involved in this at all! But I can't let you go anywhere now that you know."

She unlocked the door and pushed Elizabeth through it into the deep, dark water.

Elizabeth tumbled into the water that engulfed the lower part of the staircase. She flailed around for a moment, her eyes wide and disoriented, until she got her bearings.

"Lizzie," Jessica said, reaching out a hand to help pull her sister from the water. "It's drier up here." Most of the cheerleaders were huddling together on the top few steps—a cold, wet mass against a locked door.

"The water's rising quickly," Elizabeth said, looking around. "There isn't much time."

"How did you know we were here?" Jessica asked.

Elizabeth shook her head. "I didn't until a few minutes ago. I only came because I learned Ms. Swanson was the missing cheerleader from 1976. I didn't know I'd find you here too! Is everyone OK?"

"No," Maria said. "Poor Heather is the worst off. She's weak and running a high fever."

"Where is she?" Elizabeth asked.

"On the top step," Amy said. "Jade and Annie are watching out for her."

"How's everyone else?"

"Hungry," said Maria. "Especially Amy and Jade. They've been here since Friday without food. Jade's having dizzy spells."

"Friday?" Elizabeth asked. "Didn't anyone notice they were gone?"

"Don't ask," Patty said. "It's a long, sordid tale."

"Speaking of sordid tales, the entire town thinks you girls have been at Maria's house since yesterday, partying up a storm!" Elizabeth told them. "All over Sweet Valley parents and school officials are debating whether you guys should be grounded just for this life or for multiple reincarnations."

"Does that mean what I think it means?" Lila asked.

"I'm afraid so," Elizabeth said. "It means nobody's searching for you."

"But you brought along reinforcements—right, big sis?" Jessica asked hopefully. "In another few

217

minutes Todd, Winston, and the varsity football team will storm the place and overpower Ms. Living-in-the-past. Won't they?"

Elizabeth shook her head. "Not unless they're psychic. I didn't call them."

Lila rolled her eyes. "What kind of a rescue is this?"

"An accidental one," Elizabeth replied.

"Great." Lila groaned. "Before, we were eight teenage girls at the mercy of an armed lunatic. Now we're still at her mercy, but there are nine of us. Well, that's progress."

"At least we won't be caught short if we want to set up a baseball team," Maria quipped.

"Anyone for water polo?" asked Patty.

"Liz, what's that you're holding?" Jessica asked.

Elizabeth looked at her hand, surprised. "Some old trophy I picked up upstairs. I needed something to take a swing at Ms. Swanson with, and it was handy."

Jessica grabbed it from her. "Just some old trophy?" she asked. "Liz, do you know what you've just found?"

"What?"

"The 1976 California State Cheerleading Championship Team Trophy!" Jessica read off the plaque. "Can anyone take a stab at who stole it from the school display case that year?"

"This is fascinating, I'm sure," Lila said. "But don't we have enough *current* crimes to worry about without delving back to the Dark Ages to dig up more?"

"Delving back," Elizabeth said suddenly. "That is what we have to do."

"Come again?" Jessica asked.

"The problem is that being around cheerleaders has brought Nancy back to a time when the Girls of Seventy-six treated her cruelly because of her disability," Elizabeth said. "She thinks you're the ones who betrayed her."

"We keep telling her we're not!" Lila said. "Why can't she just take our word for it?"

"It's not that simple," Amy said. "They destroyed her self-image by forcing her off the team. And they made it hard for her to trust other people too."

"So Amy finally found a situation where she can talk the hot line speak and not irritate everyone!" Jessica observed.

"In case you guys haven't noticed, the water's four feet deep now even on the top step," Patty pointed out. Annie and Jade were standing with Heather, holding her up between them. But Heather obviously needed to be in a hospital. "We're running out of time!"

"I could knock on the door and ask Nancy's inner child to come out to play," Maria offered.

"That is exactly what we're going to do!" Elizabeth exclaimed.

Maria rolled her eyes. "Liz, it was a joke."

"I think I see what Liz is getting at," Amy said. "More than anything else, Nancy considers herself a cheerleader. It's a total part of who she is, like Liz being a writer or Lila being—"

"*Rich*," Lila supplied.

"When they took away her cheerleading, they

took away her self-image," Elizabeth mused. "Maybe we can undo that if we find a way to let her be a part of the squad again. She needs to feel needed."

"Whatever," Lila said. "I'll try anything if it will get me back in my own bed. What do we do?"

"How about we practice one of the cheers Nancy taught us?" Jessica suggested. "Just the words. And we beg her to do it with us, telling her how much we need her."

"Remember, the whole point is to get her to open that door," Elizabeth explained.

"OK, girls," Jessica shouted. "I know nobody feels much like cheering, but it just might get us out of here. Everyone do the Spirit cheer with me:

We've got the spirit! We've got the right!
We're gonna win the game tonight!
We've got the talent; we've got the heat!
Sweet Valley High's the team to beat!

"That was totally pathetic, people," Jessica complained. "We just proved that Elizabeth and I know the cheer. The rest of you hardly even tried!"

"We're scared and cold!" Maria said tearfully. Only her head was still sticking out of the water. "What do you expect?"

"This is our last chance!" croaked a weak, thin voice.

"Heather!" Elizabeth cried. "Come on, guys. If

Heather's willing to try this instead of giving up, I think the rest of us can give it our best shot too."

"She's right!" Jessica called. "Come on. Let's do it again. With conviction this time!"

We've got the spirit! We've got the right!
We're gonna win the game tonight!
We've got the talent; we've got the heat!
Sweet Valley High's the team to beat!

"Much better!" Elizabeth said. "But Lila, I still can't hear you. Let's all do it again, loud enough so Nancy can hear it over Bob Dylan."

We've got the spirit! We've got the right!
We're gonna win the game tonight!
We've got the talent; we've got the heat!
Sweet Valley High's the team to beat!

"Great!" Jessica told the squad. "But it needs something different. It needs to be . . . more personalized. Help me out here, Liz!"

"Matt Owens and Pete Winchell—no, Winchell won't work," Elizabeth said. "How about this? I'm giving you the names of some midseventies SVH football players I came across in the yearbooks. Stick them into the third line like this: 'We've got Matt Owens. We've got Big Pete.'"

"You're brilliant, Liz!" Jessica said. "Here we go, with Matt and Pete."

We've got the spirit! We've got the right!
We're gonna win the game tonight!
We've got Matt Owens! We've got Big Pete!
Sweet Valley High's the team to beat!

"I hear footsteps in the next room!" Jade said. But she began to cough, and a moment later her head disappeared under the water. Patty grabbed her shoulders and pulled her up again.

"Lila! You're tall," Patty cried. "Help me with Jade. She's fainted!"

"Everyone else keep cheering!" Jessica instructed. "I mean it!"

"But Jade—" Maria protested.

"Jessica's right. Ch-Cheer!" Heather ordered, her voice weak but full of determination.

We've got the spirit! We've got the right!
We're gonna win the game tonight!
We've got Matt Owens! We've got Big Pete!
Sweet Valley High's the team to beat!"

There was a pounding on the door. "Stop it!" Nancy screamed. "You noisy girls are making too much noise! Quiet now!"

"No, Nancy!" Jessica called. "We need you to cheer with us!" She began the cheer again, and the other girls joined in.

Individually most of the girls were weakening fast, Elizabeth knew. But together their voices were loud and strong. "Come to our cheerleading practice, Nancy!" Elizabeth urged. "It's not the same without you on the squad!"

Jessica started in on the cheer once more, and every girl shouted the words as loudly as she could.

The footsteps came closer.

"You're one of us, Nancy," Amy shouted. "You're a cheerleader! Come cheer with us."

Elizabeth motioned for Jessica to lead the cheer once more. Then Elizabeth took a deep breath and played her trump card. "George is here, Nancy! He's waiting for you! He still loves you! He wants you back!"

For a moment the only sound was the gurgling of water.

"George?" Nancy called from outside the door. "I don't believe you. You always lie. Loretta stole George from me."

The water was too deep to stand in now. Even the taller girls were treading water, but few of them were strong enough to keep it up for long.

Heather faltered and would have gone down in the dark water if Jessica hadn't wrapped an arm around her shoulders and kept her afloat.

"Nancy?" Heather shouted. "This is Loretta! We're telling you the truth about George. I never should have tried to steal him from you! It was all a mistake. You're the one George loves. Only you!" Her energy spent, she began to slide beneath the surface, but Elizabeth grasped her other shoulder.

For a moment there was no response from Nancy,

and Elizabeth was afraid their ploy had failed. Then the dead bolt slid in its groove and the door opened just a crack.

Elizabeth grinned wearily. That was all the water needed. Hundreds of gallons streamed out, wrenching open the door and knocking Nancy across the room. Her gun flew from her hand, and Elizabeth grabbed it as she gushed out with the water.

The girls were safe. And free.

Twenty minutes later Jessica sat on the front porch, wrapped in a blanket, and watched while police officers, reporters, and relieved parents swarmed all over Nancy Swanson's lawn.

Brad sauntered over to Jessica. For once she didn't care that a gorgeous guy was seeing her looking filthy and horrible.

"I guess you had quite an adventure," he said with that lazy, sexy grin that would have turned Jessica's bones to jelly—if she weren't too numb to know if she still had any bones.

"You know me," she replied. "Always up for an adventure." She knew now that she wasn't actually interested in Brad. But a little flirting never hurt. Especially when the guy was both cute and rich.

"Maybe we can make you the star of this story as well as the cheerleading one," Brad said.

"This story?" Jessica asked. "Is this a story?"

"Psycho Teacher Terrorizes High-School Cheerleading Squad? I'll say it's a story! Diane's editor will flip! Especially when it's accompanied by my outstanding examples of photojournalism."

Heather stepped out of the house, flanked by two police officers. They settled her in an armchair, wrapped in blankets, to wait for the ambulance. Brad was on her in an instant. "Hey, baby," he said. "I never would have thought a girl could look so good after what you've been through."

Behind his back Heather rolled her eyes at Jessica. They both knew they wouldn't be winning any beauty pageants that night.

Elizabeth was in the yard, speaking with a police detective. She nodded to the woman and hurried up the porch steps to Jessica. "They'll be bringing out Nancy Swanson in a minute," she said.

"Elizabeth!" Brad called. He gave her a quick peck on the forehead. "I hope you're not helping Diane write this story," he said. "After all, you're the heroine this time. It would be a conflict of interest." He gestured from Elizabeth to Jessica. "You know, Wakefields, I can never quite decide which one of you is more gorgeous. In some cultures it's acceptable for a man to court and even marry two sisters. There's this Pacific island—"

"Brad! What are you doing?" Diane yelled. "You're missing the shot!"

Brad jumped at least a foot in the air, Jessica guessed as she stood up to get a better view. Officers were already escorting Nancy down the front steps toward a waiting police car. She had her hands cuffed behind her back and a timid, bewildered expression on her face. Her left cheek was twitching furiously. Cameras flashed around her. But not Brad's. He yanked wildly at his lens cap, fiddled with the lens, and adjusted the focus. But just as he was about to snap the picture, an officer blocked his view to guide Nancy into the car.

Diane stalked over to Brad and dragged him around the side of the wraparound porch. The girls on the front porch couldn't help but overhear the conversation.

"I swear, Brad, you are not to look at a single girl for the rest of this assignment! I mean it. Maybe you don't care if I tell your father. But you'll care plenty if I tell your girlfriend!"

"Give me a break," Brad said. "It's lonely on the road."

Diane's voice was incredulous. "When have you had time to get lonely?"

"None of them meant anything to me! I was just having fun!"

Jessica was shaken, though she'd felt exactly the same way about her dates with him. She stared at Elizabeth and Heather. "I can't believe I made such stupid decisions all week for a disgusting jerk like that. We didn't mean a thing to each other! And I could have died because of it!" Her voice got very quiet. "All of us almost died."

Heather nodded. "I know exactly what you mean."

"Some things are more important than guys," Jessica decided. She enveloped Heather and

Elizabeth in a three-way hug. For now she was content just to be with family and friends.

Todd arrived at the scene a few minutes later and asked Elizabeth if they could talk privately. She guided him around to the side porch where Diane had chewed out Brad.

"I'm sorry I stood you up after basketball practice this afternoon," Elizabeth said. She stopped a moment, amazed. "Wow, was that only this afternoon? So much has happened since then!"

"I assume standing me up had something to do with speeding over here and rescuing eight kidnapped cheerleaders."

"Something like that," Elizabeth told him.

Todd wrapped both arms around her from behind. "Then I'd look like a real jerk if I held it against you, wouldn't I?"

"Probably," Elizabeth agreed.

He turned her around to face him, and he hugged her close. "Then how about if I just hold myself against you instead?"

"That would be perfect." Elizabeth sighed.

"Oh, Liz, do you have any idea how worried I was about you? I can't believe I wasted so much energy last week on that ridiculous argument. I don't even remember what I was mad about."

"Me neither," she said. "Let's never ever have another fight."

"You took the words right out of my mouth."

Epilogue

A week later *Scoop* magazine hit the newsstands. Mrs. Wakefield brought home a stack of copies, and the family pored over them at the dinner table.

"I'm psyched!" Jessica said. "Who'd have believed they would put our cheerleading squad on the cover of the whole magazine! Liz, we're famous!"

Elizabeth laughed. "And who would've believed that a simple little where-are-they-now piece would escalate into a multiple-kidnapping story?"

"What do you think of the picture, Mom and Dad?" Jessica asked. "My hair doesn't look *too* disgusting, does it?"

"It's a beautiful shot of you both," Mrs. Wakefield said.

Mr. Wakefield leaned across the table toward Jessica. "Jessica, in sixteen years I can honestly say I've never once thought your hair looked disgusting."

"Your hair looks perfect," Mrs. Wakefield assured her, passing a plate of cold cuts around. "But what's wrong, Liz? I doubt *you're* worried about your hair."

"Nothing's wrong," Elizabeth explained. "But it's just my luck. Here I am on the cover of a national magazine—and I'm wearing a cheerleading uniform! Rah-rah-rah!"

"Don't be a party pooper!" Jessica ordered, gesturing with a carrot stick. "You deserve to be on that cover as much as any of us. You were part of the number-two squad in the nation! And I bet we'll be the number-one squad now that Heather and I don't hate each other."

Elizabeth started assembling a sandwich. "I'm excited about the magazine," she said. "It's just that the cover photo was a bit of a surprise."

"I see you got your 'research assistance by Elizabeth Wakefield' credit line," Mrs. Wakefield said. "Congratulations."

"Even Winston gets to be famous!" Elizabeth exclaimed. She turned to a photograph of Nancy being led out of her house by police.

"It's a good thing Winston happened to have

his camera in his backpack when he came for Maria that night," Jessica said. "Brad totally blew that photo opportunity!"

"Dad, is there any word around the courthouse about whether Nancy's case will go to trial?" Elizabeth asked.

"The psych evaluations aren't completed yet, but I doubt she'll ever see a courtroom," Mr. Wakefield told her.

Elizabeth nodded. "Good."

Jessica raised her eyebrows. "You think it's good that she's not going to prison after what she did?"

"She's clearly not competent to stand trial," Elizabeth said. "The poor woman can't tell from one moment to the next whether it's still today or whether she's been caught in a time warp and transported back to 1976."

"Nancy doesn't exactly have a talent for reality," Jessica conceded. "What'll happen to her?"

Mr. Wakefield lifted a ceramic pitcher of ice water and poured a glass for himself. At Mrs. Wakefield's signal he poured her one as well. "My guess is long-term treatment at an institution that's equipped to handle people like her."

"People whose hobbies include drowning cheerleaders?" Jessica asked.

"Exactly," he replied with a smile. He held

up the pitcher. "Would either of you like some water?"

"*No!*" Jessica and Elizabeth yelled together.

BANTAM BOOKS TEMPT YOU TO TURN BACK TIME AND
DISCOVER A SECRET SIDE TO THE WAKEFIELD TWINS,
THE TRUTH! NEVER COMPLETELY KNOWN BEFORE –
UNTIL NOW!

SWEET VALLEY HIGH™

created by Francine Pascal

JESSICA'S SECRET DIARY

Jessica . . . the untold story

Dear Diary,
     I'm leaving home. I can't stand it anymore. Elizabeth
stole the man I love. I've lost everything to her. I hate being a
twin. I hate always being compared to perfect Elizabeth.
     Only you know, Diary, just how much she's taken from
me. After tonight, I'm sorry I went behind Elizabeth's back with
Jeffrey French. I'm not sorry about any of the things I did to her.
     Good-bye, Sweet Valley. From now on Jessica
Wakefield is going to be one of a kind!

Read all about Jessica's agonizing dilemma in this special edition
featuring classic moments from Sweet Valley High™ books 30 to 40.

The first volume of Jessica's tantalizing secret diaries.

ISBN: 0-553-40866-6

FANCY A PRIVATE GLIMPSE INTO THE DIARY OF
ANOTHER? READ ON . . .

SWEET VALLEY HIGH™

created by Francine Pascal

ELIZABETH'S SECRET DIARY

Elizabeth . . . the untold story

Dear Diary,

Todd and I are finished! I've never been more
miserable in my life. It all started when I found a letter on his
desk from a girl in Vermont. It sounded more than friendly, if you
know what I mean. I should trust Todd, but he didn't make things
better by getting mad at me for being a snoop (as he put it).

I know what you're thinking, Diary. I have no right to
complain. When Todd was gone, I let Nicholas Morrow kiss me. I
even fell in love with Jeffrey French. But Todd doesn't know the
worst. Only you, Diary, know the true story of what happened
between Todd's best friend, Ken Matthews, and me.

Read all about Elizabeth's steamy affair in this special edition
featuring classic moments from Sweet Valley High™ books 20 to 30.

The first volume of Elizabeth's tantalizing secret diaries.

ISBN: 0-553-40927-1

SWEET VALLEY UNIVERSITY™

Created by Francine Pascal

Ask your bookseller for any titles you have missed. The Sweet Valley University series is published by Bantam Books.